The Deep End

ISBN: 978-0-6151-6781-7

also by this author

Freak

Signature

Microcosmia

Carnival

Moth In The Fist

Hero

ronsandersartofprose@yahoo.com

ronsandersatwork.com

The Deep End

Savage Glen

On that lovely day Fate dumped me in the Glen I certainly had it coming, but, given my state of mind at the time, probably wouldn't have sidestepped even if I'd been tipped off to the grisly outcome.

I was a homeless, penniless, self-absorbed drifter. My shirt and trousers were grimy and riddled with holes, my hair tangled and unshorn. My toes, nine funky creatures that were bleeding and gnarled, poked numbly from their torn canvas homes. To top it off I smelled like a cesspool, and knew it. But I was way beyond stares and whispers, deaf to the clack of quickly locked latches, unmoved by the sight of glaring mothers. Man, I was so far gone the gulls laughed as they pelted my hair and shoulders.

I'd been working my way back down the Monterey coastline, having not seen a job or a Jackson since San Diego, maybe a year ago. My worldly possessions consisted of an old transistor radio with a dead battery, a broken hairbrush, and a pair of binoculars I'd picked up beachcombing; all kept rolled in a ratty, malodorous sleeping bag. Physically, even at this advanced stage of moral deterioration, I could have taken the necessary steps to redeem myself, but lately a particularly vile bile had come to roost in my soul. Ambition, wonder, compassion—these things were all but strangers to me. And as for the cozy, gaily motoring Beautiful People, they could go straight to Hell for all I cared. Nothing mattered any more.

Sometimes I'd hitchhike, sometimes I'd walk up or down the coast highway making camp wherever my fancy dictated. Recently I'd taken to wandering along the sand in Monterey's quaint beach communities, back and forth, day after day, until some bored lifeguard or other chased me off. I never gave anybody a hard time; I'd simply nod and split. Anywhere was as good as anywhere else.

But today, as I sat on a jumble of rocks off the promenade watching the fat sun set, I was in no mood to be pushed. My stomach was rumbling and writhing, my joints ready to seize, my hands and feet freezing. All I needed was some tightwad freak to wish me a nice day. To my right, the endless beach was quickly succumbing to twilight, and to my left a commercial pier stood over the waves like a tentative centipede, its underbelly secured from the public by a sturdy chain link fence. Behind this fence bunched a solid green jungle of lady fern, so densely packed it must have grown unchecked for years. On the boardwalk above were a small parking lot, an amusement arcade, a bait and tackle shop, a diner, and, just at the boardwalk's entrance, a little market which also did business in funshine souvenirs. The market's outer walls sported a continuous mural of long shapely ferns and pussy willows under a washed azure sky. Peeking from this idyllic dreamscape were leggy fawns, reddish-brown monarchs, smiling squirrels and carefree jays. A sign above the mural, bearing script as fanciful as the painting, read *GENTLE GLEN*. Only a few people were patronizing the place, but I knew it was where I'd be bumming my dinner. As I sat scoping it out, a curly blonde in cutoffs and frilly white blouse approached an exiting customer and began gesticulating and touching. The man—a very burly, swarthy character in Bermudas, windbreaker, and fedora—smiled and ran an arm around her waist. After a few more words they began sauntering across the parking lot. A minute later another man appeared at the door, wearing a white apron and sour expression. He watched them leaning on the rail for a bit, looking as though he would spit, then reached to the inner wall and switched on the market's corner floodlights. I shook my head and creaked to my feet. When it came to making a buck some people were born with a distinct advantage.

Once the aproned man was back inside I picked my way over the rocks, ambled up to the market and leaned against the front wall out of the floods' glare. No one going in or out felt compelled to offer me anything other than a hard look. I was just reaching the point where hunger makes panhandling aggressive when my radar warned of an approaching cold front. That man in the white apron came back out and fixed me with a very tough stare. "No offense—" he began.

"But take a hike. Right?"

"Right."

"Just going." I bent to lift my sleeping bag, my knees and back protesting, my head swimming. I was hurting for protein. The man in the apron disappeared. Before I could leave he reappeared with a squashed cold sandwich. "Maybe this'll tide you over."

"But don't come back. Right?"

"Right."

I thanked him and slunk around the market to a wall facing the parking lot, peeling off the cellophane with my teeth. We both knew I'd be back. It was growing dark, so I sat against the market's west wall under an epileptic floodlight. I was just getting comfortable when that same curly blonde came hurrying across the parking lot, looking scared. Spotting me, she rushed right up.

"'*Scuse* me," she burst out, "but if it's okay could I, like, just *stand* here with you? Just for a little while? There's some guy back there who's really giving me a hard time. He'll back off if he sees I'm not alone."

I shrugged and tore into my sandwich. Bologna. It figured. Now I could see that she was closer to forty than thirty, and that makeup couldn't hide the wear and tear on her psyche. But she must have been really pretty in her day, before the crow's feet and stress lines did their number on her face. She kept looking back at the row of cars, where a dark figure leaned on the rail overlooking the beach.

"Doesn't look like he's going anywhere soon," I remarked, finishing off my sandwich. Half a minute passed. She was starting to bug me. "Why don't you go ask the guy in the market to call you a cop or something?"

"He don't specially like me," she said, sitting way too close. "I'm not real popular around the Glen."

I crushed the cellophane into a ball and looked away.

"My name's Cici," she breathed. "My friends call me Peaches." She squinted at the cars. The dark figure was getting bolder, moving our way a yard at a time. "C'mon," Cici said urgently. "Walk with me a ways, will you?"

"Walk where?" And suddenly I picked up on an old vibe. This whole deal smelled of a setup.

"Just to where we can get away from this guy, okay? I've got a place he don't know about—nobody knows about it. We can ditch him. Look, I'm *hip* to this dude, okay? He's real dangerous." She took my arm.

"What's all this 'we' stuff? Since when did we become partners?"

"Would you just *come on*, already!" The dark figure was ambling our way. I groaned to my feet and grabbed my sleeping bag, intending to separate myself from the proceedings gruffly and with finality, but Cici, a no-nonsense grip on my arm, surprised me by dragging me around the market toward the pier's arched entrance. The dark figure began to follow in earnest.

"Look," I said, attempting to extract my arm, "just get out of your own jams, all right? I got problems of my own." Everything was happening too fast.

"*Shut up!*" Cici hissed. "*Down here!*" She pulled me around the railing onto the sand. It was fully dark now, and my heart was pounding. What was I going to do, use a transistor radio to fight off some horny pissed goon? Cici hurried me alongside the fence to a spot maybe twenty feet from the waterline. There the fence continued at a right angle, leaving beachgoers plenty of room to walk below. Glancing over my shoulder as we ducked underneath, I saw a black form jumping onto the sand.

"Jesus!" I tried yanking out my arm, but Cici wasn't buying. At that I realized it wasn't some kind of setup after all. She was just as scared.

"Quick!" she whispered. "In here!"

Now I'll have to be absolutely clear in my description, because I still get confused when I recall how we worked our way into that place. Cici led me around a soggy wooden pillar and behind a clump of tall, sour-smelling plants. We stepped up on a tiny wood platform, scooted around another pillar and squeezed behind a row of heavy standing planks, took a few paces toward the water on a sagging beam. She parted another clump of those plants to reveal a cut section of chain link fence. The section swung inward at her push, and I followed her in. The fence swung shut behind me. We were up to our ankles in chilly sand, completely engulfed by those plants.

Cici put a finger to my lips. *"Shhh!"*

It wasn't at all dark, for long white slats from the pier's security floodlights shone through the boardwalk's interstices. In a moment we could hear somebody run past, pause, and continue running.

Cici took my hand and led me down a snaking path hacked through the foliage. Its density amazed me. The place was a weird, groping jungle; a hidden world.

We came to a clearing where three men as grungy as I sat around a gallon jug of cheap red wine. Considerable work had gone into making the place a home. Sodden pillars bore slats nailed horizontally to serve as shelves for found bric-a-brac, walkways had been laid using large stones and cinder blocks, crude walls were fashioned of hung plywood scraps. Tacked to these walls were a few posters, a wall clock without hands, a three-years-old calendar. Strategically placed chairs and mattresses showed half in shadow.

The man to my right rose as soon as we came into the open. Not only did he have the look of an obnoxious and felonious bully, there were aspects of his expression which gave an impression of real viciousness, perhaps even psychosis. He was physically big, and broad, and of a pasty complexion that vaguely came off as diseased, but more striking by far was the fact that he was absolutely *hairless*—and not merely shaven.

There wasn't a trace of hair on his face, upper chest, or arms, not an eyelash or brow hair; and all this was evident from ten yards away. Several tattoos showed loudly against the whiteness of his flesh, one in particular—the realistically depicted, and strategically placed, scars of a hangman's noose—plainly intended to shock and intimidate. "Who the hell's that?" were the first words out of his mouth.

"*That*," Cici retorted, half-whispering, "is a friend of mine. We was being chased by Otto." I was to learn that almost all verbal exchanges were served up sotto voce in this place. She marched us right up to the little group, pulled a twenty from her bra, and held it triumphantly under the hairless man's nose. "You know how he acts when he don't get his way. We had to ditch him."

The big guy tore the bill out of Cici's hand and stuck a forefinger in her face. "How many times I got to tell you nobody comes in the Glen without my okay?" He gave me a really bad news look meant to scare the hell out of me, but I just ignored him and continued looking around. Maybe he wasn't used to confronting people who didn't care any more.

He tried that hard look again, shook his head and muttered, "Funky-assed hooker."

The guy sitting to my left was filthy and heavyset, wearing gray sweatpants, tennis shoes, an enormous overcoat, a black beret. Horn-rimmed spectacles with exceedingly thick lenses caused his eyes to appear offset. He winked and said genially, "Now as you're native, comfort your bones and draw with us one."

I snapped, *"What?"* wondering if I was being put on.

"Siddown and have a drink," Cici interpreted.

"And another thing," the big guy rasped. "You quit turning tricks out front, okay? I told you once already you're gonna blow it for us. Keep your butt up on the pier."

"And, Ci'," the genial man piped, "may I be first to express our gratitude concerning the wherewithal for this night's repast."

The big guy grabbed the fellow in the middle and yanked him to his feet. "Elf, you go upstairs and get some grub. Bread, cuts, and cheese. And another jug of grape." Elf, who looked like his moniker, took the bill sheepishly.

The heavyset man groaned. "*Pleeease.* Not port; not again." He rubbed a pudgy hand on his ample belly. "Mine ulcer, she sings."

The big guy glared. *"Grape!"*

Elf nodded and made his way out, looking haunted.

I sat and accepted the jug, half-tempted to follow Elf out. But there was something about the big man's manner that made me do the one thing that would really gore him. Casually sipping wine, I made a show of getting cozy.

"You ain't wanted here!" he said, reading my mind. He strode through the foliage and disappeared behind a ramshackle partition.

Cici, sitting right beside me, said, "Best you don't challenge him too much. He's not just rowdy, he's really off his nut. Once he told me he's been like, you know, confined. For hurting somebody bad. And I seen him turn weird, if you know what I mean. He gets this look in his eyes like...*wow!* And he carries this great big hunting knife he likes to flash around, which he says he can't wait to use on some big mouth. But most of the time he just gets his way with his fists." She pulled back a handful of curls, revealing an ear that was swollen and discolored. "That's what he done to me yesterday. And no reason, neither. Just out of the blue."

I glanced at her ear and looked away. I'd seen worse. "Looks like it's about time you elected yourselves a new big cheese."

The bespectacled man sighed. "No Constitution down here, amigo. It's the law of the jungle, both figuratively and literally. And sweet old Animal's no more guilty of being human than the rest of us."

I grunted. "Animal. I would've guessed something more like Monster." The ferns all seemed to lean to the clearing, eavesdropping. I found myself whispering. "Groovy little setup you've got yourselves here. Kinda reminds be of a place I once saw in a picture book. Borneo, I think it was called."

The man sighed again. *"Athyrium filix-foemina,"* he moaned. "Californicum Butters. Likes it shady and moist." He glanced around meaningfully. "Obviously."

"Crap grass," Cici translated.

My eyes were adjusting to the contrasts of light and shadow. "What's this Animal guy's hold around here, anyway? Never before met a man I disliked so much so fast."

"Rule by terror," the bespectacled man said. "Gets his way with a gesture or a grimace." He tossed his head. "Alopecia, along with a heavy dose of incarceration, may have played telling roles in his present behavior. But he's too hung up to realize it's not necessary. Here he bides, cohabiting with three of the gentlest folk you'd ever hope to meet, and still he swaggers around like there's a mutiny threatening his little fiefdom. But it's all a lark to me. I'm easy." He smiled and offered his dry old hand. "Name's Ollen. Ollen Keats Farthingsworth III. That seems a little prolix in present company, so I just go by 'the Poet'."

I nodded curtly. I'd always seen a handshake as an empty ritual; in more cases than not an invitation to a double-cross.

The Poet smiled again. "Like I said, I'm easy." There was a whisper of brushed fronds as Elf slithered in, a bulky shopping bag in the crook of his arm. He extracted a gallon jug of port, a loaf of French bread, a package of cheese slices, and some cold cuts wrapped in white butcher's paper.

Animal must have been listening for him, for he reappeared and strode right up, tore the food and wine out of Elf's hands and sat cross-legged with it all tucked between his knees. He stuffed the change in his shirt's pocket, ripped the loaf down the center and crammed in the cheese and cold cuts. Without a word he began wolfing down the enormous sandwich, starting in the middle and working toward both ends. The bully was reestablishing his domain.

Animal made a point of hogging the meal solely to get to me. Suddenly, mid-swallow, his eyes rose and burned directly into mine. The man was so loathsome I couldn't help returning the stare with venom, and as our eyes locked everything around us seemed to freeze. Only as those ugly eyes grew progressively viler did I realize I'd been trapped into staring down a psychopath. Without averting his gaze Animal completed the swallow and slowly and pointedly rubbed the uneaten portion in the sand between his knees. At the corner of my vision I saw Elf's face fall.

Still holding my eyes, Animal made a show of reaching under his shirt. He drew out his hunting knife and slowly brandished it at eye level. I could tell how big the thing was without having to look at it directly, and while our little contest went on and on he twirled the blade in his fingers, catching and passing the radiance from the floods above. The whole point of this gambit wasn't to frighten me, but to break my stare with reflected light.

"Ahem," said the Poet.

No one moved. I realized I didn't have a thing to gain by beating Animal at his game, but I was already in too far. The more menacing his stare became, the more stolid I made mine. Crazy as it sounds, this must have gone on for the better part of an hour. Cici, Elf, and the Poet fidgeted as I willed myself to stone. At length sweat began to creep over Animal's forehead. His eyelids twitched. I saw him blink twice, almost imperceptibly. The man's mouth twisted into a bitter snarl, his eyelids fluttered, his face began to quake. He grunted and, his eyes still married to mine, took a vicious swipe at my face with the blade. The tip just brushed my cheek, not quite breaking the skin.

The Poet was first to react. "Under the circumstances," he breathed, "mayhaps mine ulcer wouldst not complain all that vociferously." He gingerly plucked the jug from between Animal's legs, unscrewed the cap and drank his fill. Elf and Cici responded like children under a Christmas tree, fidgeting and giggling. They nervously passed the jug.

Animal ignored them. Our eyes remained locked, his expression even meaner than before.

"Look!" Cici squealed. "Look at the lights! Somebody's turned on the arcade!"

Someone above, the electrician apparently, had indeed lit the amusement arcade's parti-colored neon façade, and now ghostly primary and secondary spots were dancing about us, vanishing and reappearing between the pillars and ferns. The effect was extremely surreal.

"Like being in a snow bubble," Elf tittered. "You know, one of those little glass things you turn upside-down and shake."

Just as suddenly the effect passed, leaving only the stark, humorless spears from the floodlights.

"Shoot!" Cici pouted. "Somebody had to go and turn us rightside-up again!"

The Poet chuckled. "Never in a day," spake he, "hast one's going wit so trod the moment made."

"Shut up," said Animal.

The Poet looked at him quizzically, a patient smile on his face. "Meaning what? Meaning let the bearing quiet run the clockwork of our lives? Meaning fault the Muse for sorrow's sake, that our—"

"Meaning shut your stupid face," Animal said menacingly. "I'm sick of listening to your crap, you got me? So either you clam up or I'm gonna clam you up. Is that clear enough for you?"

"We need not evoke bivalves," the Poet responded in all seriousness, "nor the product of our bowels. If perchance mine song should ring askance—"

"I said," Animal screamed, *"shut up!"*

The Poet stared for a long minute, blinking. Wine had made him careless, and a bit slow on the uptake. He looked at us uncertainly, wondering if his speech was garbled. The faces returning his stare were white as death. The Poet turned back to Animal. *"Believe* me," he began, "lest I seem remiss in endeavoring to—"

What happened next happened so fast and so unexpectedly we were all struck dumb. Animal grabbed the Poet by the hair, yanked his head forward, and slit his throat in one clean swipe. The Poet gawked at the blood spurting on his overcoat. His hand started for his throat, but before it could make it he pitched forward. I sat quietly, bespattered, watching the spurts taper until the Poet was no more. Cici was in a strange posture, her hands raised, her eyes wide, her mouth all agape. I kind of expected a cinematic, piercing scream, but what came out was more like a tea kettle's piping. And, like a kettle's song, the sound just went on and on, finally descending in pitch until it blew away as a sigh.

"Jeez, Animal," Elf whispered. *"Jeez,* man!"

Animal glared maniacally, waiting for me to move. I couldn't tell if he was smiling or snarling, but I wasn't about to stare him down this time.

"Dump him," Animal told Elf, his eyes pursuing mine. "In the back."

Elf wobbled to his feet. "I—I can't lift him. He's too heavy." He sounded like he was about to break into tears. "What'd you have to go and do that for, Animal?" He turned to me with a look of supplication.

"In the back," Animal repeated.

Elf turned to Cici, whose eyes were rolling round and round in her head, then back to me. "Help me out," he whined, "huh, guy?" But I knew enough to sit tight. Animal's stare was searing.

Elf dragged the Poet's body through the foliage, making an awful lot of noise. In a few minutes we heard him whimpering maybe thirty feet away, and eventually the sounds of digging.

Animal hefted the near-full jug and tilted back his head, his eyes never leaving mine. He swallowed and swallowed, his face contorting. I knew this wasn't for show, he really needed that drink. At last he lowered the jug and secured it between his thighs. There was a long silence, broken only by Elf's distant whining and by Animal's heavy breathing. Cici's eyes avoided us both, and mine were fixed on Animal's knife. In my heart I knew he was waiting for an excuse—any excuse—to use it on me, and that he was only beginning to consider the enormity of his crime. Animal belched, feigning calm. It didn't take a psychoanalyst to figure out what he was up to. He was using the alcohol to steel himself, realizing he now had three witnesses to deal with.

The pier creaked and trembled with the tide as the tension wound down. Animal played out his scene with the jug, his eyes glazing, his mouth hanging open for successively longer intervals. I saw a ray of hope. If the big man managed to drink himself silly I could walk.

At last he set down the jug, having killed well over half. He stared dully at Cici and slowly moved his hand to stroke her hair. At his touch her eyes came to life, darting side to side, lighting on me imploringly. Animal wasn't too drunk to not pick up on her look. His attention rolled back and forth between us—it was obvious he saw her less as a sexual opportunity than as a means to provoke me. He raised the knife until it was positioned before her face.

"C'mere."

Cici didn't budge, but her eyes were all over the place. Animal grinned, casually brought the blade around to her back and used the tip to snip off her blouse's buttons one by one. He did it dispassionately, methodically, like a man removing grapefruit seeds with a butter knife.

Cici's blouse fell open. Animal used the knife's tip to draw it away from her body. Amid the spears of light and shadow the whiteness of her bra served more to accentuate than conceal her breasts. Animal rested the flat of his blade against her throat. Watching me all the while, he slid it caressingly around her neck and down her back, finally hooking it under the bra's strap. His eyes gleamed. With the gentlest flick he severed the strap. Cici shuddered as Animal used the blade to fling off her brassiere. Topless, caught in that wholly vulnerable posture amid the shadowy ferns, Cici possessed a sensuality that evoked every healthy male's wildest fantasies.

The big man's strategy was definitely working. Certain primitive urges, as protective as they were erotic, made me want to wrest that blade from him, cut out his filthy heart, and cart off my prize.

Animal smiled. "Where's your manners, boy?"

Cici watched only me as Animal pulled her face onto his lap. The knife glinted against her throat.

"I *said*," he hissed, "turn...a...*round*." I carefully turned away and stared coldly at the ferns. Animal wasn't content to make a pig of himself and be done with it; he had to rub my face over and over in his gathering show of excess. Hours were lost in a greasy blur of gulps and grunts and squeals of disgust. It was a numbing experience to have to sit there, listening helplessly while the morning light drew dreamy patterns on the plants and piling. Never had a night passed so quickly. Finally Cici gave a little sob of defeat. I heard Animal's voice say, "All right, get up."

Unbidden, I turned back around. Animal was hitting the jug again, looking glum, and Cici was on her feet, naked, staring at a point equidistant between us. Animal almost lost his balance pulling up his pants. Cici turned to face me directly, caught in the classic pose of feminine abashment: right forearm covering the breasts, left hand concealing the crotch, right knee turned in. Then a really strange thing happened. She let her arms drop to her sides and looked me straight in the eye. My pulse shimmied at the mixed signals.

Animal took another long swallow, looking anything but triumphant, his drunken gaze languishing on Cici's stance. He blearily studied the way she was watching me, filled his mouth with wine, leaned forward and spat the mouthful in my face. I let the wine roll into my eyelashes and off my chin, refusing to react. He ticked the knife back and forth before me, very slowly, like a metronome's pendulum set to largo. "I got eyes," he said, and his face shook a bit. "Okay, tough guy. *You* do her, then."

I forced myself to not tense up, still waiting for that subtle drift of countenance that would show he'd overextended himself with the wine. But his size seemed to be working in his favor. Drunk as he was, he didn't appear anywhere near losing it. "Up!" he said. "Get...*up!*"

Rising slowly, I prepared to make my break. Again Animal seemed to read my mind. He grabbed Cici's calf and tenderly stuck the blade's tip in her navel. "Get your duds off— *now!*"

I kicked away my shoes, peeled off my shirt, dropped my pants and shorts. Cici and I stood face to face, our bodies inches apart. Only then did she begin to weep. The sound was soft as a whisper. I looked past her.

Animal swallowed and swallowed, set the jug down hard. He began tapping the blade against the glass, enjoying himself. The jug was almost empty.

"And," I said quietly, not really sure what made me take a stand, "so help me God, pigman, when I'm done I'm gonna take that bottle and stuff it right down your bleached ugly face."

The pinging stopped. Animal was gaping up at me, his expression an odd blend of exultation and amazement. His eyes danced. "Elf!" he crowed. "Make room for another!"

"Just a little man," I went on numbly, sensing his pride, and knowing I'd already gone too far. "Just a scared little man with a big, bad knife." Animal's eyes narrowed. His face assumed that same cruel expression that had so vexed me when I came into this place. With a grunt he plunged the blade into the sand, pushed himself to his feet, and rammed Cici aside. Before I could respond he had his hands on my throat and was choking me for all he was worth.

I can't remember too much of the ensuing minute or so. I still see the shadows swirling about me as unconsciousness approached, and I still feel Animal's thumbs pressing against my windpipe, harder and harder, and I still smell his foul alcoholic breath taking away what little air I could manage. But most of all I vividly see his face up against mine. And I remember how the savageness of that expression intensified, and how it became ecstatic, only to slowly lose its flame, waning almost to a look of sadness. A fuzzy spark of *just maybe* hit me—the dying man's last gasp of hope he'll be spared by a trace of humanity. Animal's sad look declined in sync with my flagging awareness; the expression becoming regret, becoming weariness, becoming stupor as we collapsed. Through the coalescing shades of gray I caught a glimpse of Animal's hunting knife protruding between his shoulder blades, saw Cici's worried face looking into mine, and finally had a blurry impression of little Elf peering over her shoulder.

There wasn't a whole lot to be done in a constructive vein. Elf wordlessly dragged Animal's body to join the Poet's while Cici and I stood silently, finishing off what was left of the wine. In a few minutes Elf was back, Animal's hunting knife in his trembling hand.

"Only one thing to do, man," he said. "Throw this sucker in the water and hightail it out of here. No weapon, no case." He wiped the blade at his feet, encrusting it with sand. "You can just leave those guys in the back and let this stuff grow over 'em. Nobody'll ever know." He stashed the knife under his coat and looked around, searching for words. At last he said, "Man...I'm *outta* here!" and darted through the greenery.

Cici and I avoided eye contact, staring at the fronds long

after the entrance had rustled shut. My eyes, reacting to day-break, fell on the scant piles of our clothes. It was very quiet; only the murmuring of breakers and the creaking footfalls of stoic fishermen.

"Look at us," Cici said, embarrassed. "Just like Adam and Eve in the Garden of Eden." Her fingers brushed my thigh.

We faced each other, and I found myself staring frankly at her naked body. I swallowed. "Now I can see," I whispered, "why they call you Peaches." Long shafts of morning sun began to play over the foliage, bringing to life a lush and primitive arena. "Tell you what," I said, letting my hand ride down her spine, "I'll be Adam."

Why I Love Democracy

By

Enrique Batsnuwa LaCszynevitch McGomez

In researching this paper I could not help but be struck by how very much we take for granted in our wonderful country. Less than a century ago this was a different nation indeed; a nation where femepersons were unbearably repressed, where mascupersons were allowed to perpetuate their myth of gender dominance, and where demopersons of diverse ethnicity were perennially humbled and brutalized. I speak, of course, of the reign of terror concocted by that notorious agent of subjugation, that swaggering bully, the White Indigenous Male Protestant (WIMP).

Ever since the great, all-encompassing movement we know as Progressive Liberal Reform prevailed, beginning with the effective dissolution of our borders ("Illegal Alien" Anti-Discrimination Act, 2011), the changes have been sweeping and dramatic, and today it is crystal clear that the concepts *freedom* and *liberty* can only be interpreted as *absolute rights*; and that finding objectionable the behavior—no matter how egregious—of any person other than a WIMP is de facto prejudice. Now once-suspect demopersons have the run of our streets, and law enforcement walks a very fine line between apprehension and lawsuit.

But before PLR became the single, imperative interpretation of our beloved Constitution, our great nation's political atmosphere was divided into two basic camps. These two continuously bickering factions, originally known as *Democrats* and *Republicans*, grew even more estranged after the Unutterable Depression of 2033, evolving into those defunct camps still generally described as *Left Wing*, or Government Instituted for a Meaningful and Merciful Economy (GIMME), and *Right Wing*, or the Grand Old Trustee Commission for a Humane America (GOTCHA). Not until the so-called "Minority Revolt" of 2039 did the infamous conservative arm of our government see the light, disband entirely, and free itself of its barbaric ways.

To document The Transition, I hope my use of subtitles in this paper will assist in manifesting our nation's tremendous advances.

The Economics of Compassion

Our country's political progress has been nothing less than spectacular, for time and again PLRs have demonstrated just how relentlessly *caring* they can be. I could devote pages here to the dauntlessness of those liberal American femepersons, the renowned *Screaming Sheilas*, who selflessly breast-fed platypus ducklings during the Tasmanian Drought of 2019, pages more to the intrepidity of the venerated *Poor Dearers* of the 2030s, who risked life and limb to reach a golden eagle's aerie, there to nest-sit the eggs in freezing weather for days while the crippled mother recuperated, an entire document to the valor of the old *Greenpeace* organization, wiped out in a bloody confrontation with the Upper States' Yukon "eskimoes" over the Constitutional rights of the arctic char.

But the noblest case in point—and the most striking example of how even zealous PLRs can go awry—would of course be the Great Drive of 2045, when it was discovered that that rarest of rare birds, the Funnytailed Pucebreasted Slugsucker, had in fact become an endangered species. Overnight an unprecedented national campaign was undertaken on their behalf. Parades stocked with municipally-sponsored, appropriately costumed Funnytailers raised hundreds of thousands of dollars, while entrepreneurs of every sort made fortunes by dyeing their wares puce for the Conscientious Consumer. The public was *besieged* by Slugsucker minutia, over every medium, around the clock. *Millions* were raised for the birds' preservation through cuts in defense and astrophysical research, while homeowners everywhere became proud members of the nationwide Adopt a Sucker Society (ASS).

The results were fantastic, inspiring, heart-warming.

The Funnytailed Pucebreasted Slugsucker began to multiply in numbers that were absolutely staggering, their little fuzzy-faced offspring popping up in cornfields, backyards, nurseries, freighters, supermarket produce sections—you name it. However, one unfortunate consequence of this marvelous application of liberal engineering was that, with so many Slugsuckers about, the slug population began to diminish at an alarming rate, until slugs likewise became an endangered species.

Reformists lost no time.

"Save The Slugs!" they cried, *"Save The Slugs!"* and this became a Progressive Liberal anthem which galvanized the nation. Soon "Slugfests" were all the rage, and teenagers were "doing The Slime" from St. Petersburg, New Haiti to Los Angeles, New Central America. Cruising was out, oozing was in; the Ughmobile caught on like wildfire. The slug quickly became our Poster Pest, and *billions* were raised for its welfare. In no time slugs had not only made a comeback, but were absolutely ubiquitous. The slugs were happy, the Funnytailed Pucebreasted Slugsuckers were happy, Progressive Liberal Reformists were happy.

But, with a superabundance of slugs, the state of American Follaceous Health began to deteriorate at an unbelievable rate. Scarcely any leafage was safe. Finally, in a desperation move, proud Americans tightened their belts even further to finance the genetic crossbreeding of a number of supple garden strains with a hardy, fast-growing variety of African swamp grass, which was cultivated over wide areas to give the omnipresent slugs an alternate and plentiful food source.

The tragic result is known to every Liberal American schoolperson. The swamp grass trapped so much rainfall that vast areas became wetlands, the wetlands became spawning grounds for alligators, and the alligators ate all the Funnytailed Pucebreasted Slugsuckers.

"Let there be no misunderstanding here!" PuertoGeorgia senator Lolita Wang-Ho Kumba-Sanchezski said angrily as she, resplendent in Mourning Puce, confronted the Congressional Budget Committee. "Until we learn to stop throwing money away on defense programs and industry, and begin devoting more capital to the interests of meaningful domestic problems like the plight of the Funnytailed Pucebreasted Slugsucker, this kind of horror story is doomed to be repeated!"

Penal Rights

Modern, open-minded demopersons now understand that there are no bad human beings; there is only bad legislation. The realization that murderers, embezzlers, and arsonists were once actually *punished,* instead of treated with the love and compassion they deserve, still leaves many of us with an acute sense of embarrassment. This evolution—from the barbaric to the enlightened—can perhaps best be shown in the Penal Paradox Proposition, as served by Baja Louisiana senator Imran Wendell O'Mikosovitch: "They've lived lives of corruption, debauchery, promiscuousness, vandalism, indolence, socioeconomic subterfuge, compulsive predation, and, in more than a few cases, unprovoked and ungovernable savagery...and now you want to put them *in jail?* For goodness' sake, haven't they suffered enough?"

Of course, Penal Rights has always been one of the major issues of Enlightened Liberal Reform. Ps. Helga Spatsznsteinski, in her groundbreaking work, *Serial Killers Need Love, Too* correctly pointed out that an overabundance of affection can have the same adverse effect as no affection at all. For example, in the early years of reformism a number of unlucky and misguided souls—formerly disparaged as "criminals"—were forced to sue the Federal Government for the right to privacy when highly competitive and overly arduous femepersons persisted in deluging many incarcerated rapists, compulsively assaultive misogynists, and child molesters with marriage proposals. As famed debutante dismemberer Ps. Muhammed-Fritz Olgafenritz (The "Hacksmith") complained, "They only love me for my genetic makeup, not for my mind."

And just as intrusive were the lucrative contract deals from filmmakers and biographers, the unending requests for speaking engagements and intimate photo sessions, the toys-to-cologne endorsement proposals, the seemingly infinite queues of fawning dignitaries and celebrities. "Being a superstar," Ps. Gorbafyoo I. Zeimensch-Umbawi proclaimed bitterly from the Tampa Federal Resort and Spa for Violent Repeat Offenders, "just ain't what it's cracked up to be."

Even before The Transition, the curse of capital punishment was mercifully on the wane. It is now no more than a slew of ugly memories, perhaps best typified by that powerfully patriotic moment when Raul Ignacio "Little Nate" Ivenski Deng-Foo berated his executioners even as he was about to be administered that despicably *lethal* dose of HGSN (early Reformism's short-lived but well-intentioned Happy Go Sleep Now pill). Umbrageous at man's mistreatment of his fellow man, Deng-Foo heroically and famously proclaimed: "You can take away my kiddie porn! You can rob me of my drugs and electro-orifice stimulators! You can deprive me of my God-given right to whip the tar out of my children, my grandmother, and even my bichon frise, but, damn you, you'll never take away my dignity!"

Or, of course, that shocking moment when six of the early adherents of Progressive Liberal Reform burst into the "Death Chamber" and clung tearfully to convicted cannibal and rapist David Hartford's body while chanting the chorus to Danny and the Democrats' 2009 hit *Love Them Everlasting* as Hartford was insensitively murdered by society in that notorious instrument of evil, the "electric chair".

The odious death sentence's abolition ensures us all that these precious individuals live to a ripe old age with dignity and in comfort, resting assured that their constitutional rights will be adamantly protected by every attorney we liberals can possibly afford.

Semantics

Nomenclature has powerfully affected our nation's political evolution. Symbiotic Domesticile Partners, for instance, used to suffer terribly under their humiliating appellation "pets" (Faunal Emancipation Agreement, 2047). Efflorescing Abode Enhancers were finally granted the dignity they deserve by abolishing their former embarrassing cognomen "houseplants" (Floral Rights Act of 2051). In the social arena, it is now of course unthinkable that Ejaculation Engineers could actually have been demeaned as *"prostitutes"*, or that Ecobraves were once variously demeaned as *thugs, hooligans, deadbeats, junkies*, and *muggers*. Nowadays it is painfully obvious that such unfortunates would never have been forced to sink to their unhappy state had our nation previously been compassionate enough to bestow the tremendous grants they presently receive. Yet some throwback radical extremists, generously allowed by our great country to express their outmoded views, continue to point out that the more money our tax dollars provide for these poor victims, the more they indulge in the very behavior the policy is intended to alleviate.

What could more clearly demonstrate how lack of compassion can befuddle the thinking process?

These continuously suffering souls are of course martyrs, willing to maintain their grievous condition for the sake of preserving a cultural phenomenon which has long been the whipping boy of the Haves.

And even our own precious American childpersons have been the target of slurslingers. When Ps. Mongo Le Ramalama Deng-Hwong had the audacity to publish her viciously titled book, *Our Kids, Our Treasures*, the national outrage was phenomenal. "Our children are not goats!" cried millions of offended parents. Ps. Mongo LeRamalama Deng-Hwong was ostracized, and the quickly formed Attorneys Vying for Adolescent Rights Involving the Curtailment of Epithets (AVARICE) found themselves entertaining more lawsuits than they could handle.

Once we the people were made aware of the insidious subterfuge of negative semantics maintained by WIMPs, it became evident that all heterosexuals are really homophobic, and all homosexuals heterophobic; that all mascupersons are in actuality femephobic, all femepersons mascuphobic. These irrational fears and prejudices, we now understand, come from a deep underlying envy of one's *opposite pole*. Enlightened Liberal Reform has allowed us to realize that, since all persons are created constitutionally equal, one's opposite pole is in actuality one's *Natural Counterpart*. Just as mascupersons and femepersons are Natural Counterparts while being diametrically opposite in nature, so too are atheophobes ("theists") in reality the Natural Counterparts of theophobes ("atheists"). Finally, after decades of dealing with bestiphobes, dementephobes, prostiphobes, narcophobes, politiphobes, lucrephobes, penuphobes, *ad infinitum*; of legaphobes fearing crimiphobes and crimiphobes fearing legaphobes, of natuphobes living in mortal terror of urbaphobes while the urbaphobes lost sleep worrying over natuphobes; while illaphobes dwelt in horror of wellaphobes and wellaphobes locked doors against the encroachment of illaphobes; while necrephobes anguished over vitaphobes and the vitaphobes, presumably, were turning in their graves due to the necrephobes, PLRs were struggling to find a truly democratic solution. This solution eventually came to light in the national acceptance of *Phobophobia*.

Progressive Liberal Spirituality

That old paper tyrant, the "Bible", was originally sullied by references to the deity as "He". Such an obvious disparaging of femepersons was first solved by the inclusion of an "opposite-but-equal" deity, which resulted in the infamous "Mrs. God" trial of 2034. This quandary was democratically solved by the admission of an androgynous deity, the very SheHe now worshipped nationwide. Then there was the matter of the former "Old" Testament, so offensive to senior citizens—vividly expressed in the great coast-to-coast Walker Brigade. Step by step, each WIMP-enforced bias has met its demise.

And there were of course great difficulties involving religious symbolism. Public displays of Nativity scenes, stars of David, etc., have all gone the way of the dinosaur. *No single religion shall have visual dominance in our great democracy!* A "Christian nation," indeed! Our sole Yule symbol is now a giant one-eyed Buddha wearing a crown of thorns while sitting on a tortoise-shaped prayer rug before a serpent-entwined cross. From the arms of that cross dangle a crucifix, chakra, incense burner, and menorrah. And on every Nationally-Integrated Non-specific New Year's (NINNY) all we Progressive Liberal Reformists take a neutral breath in unison and "Thank Blank" that no group has cause to be offended.

Sexual Liberty

Certainly, the alienation of homosexuals has always been a tremendous social blight. Their persecution knew no bounds. So, in today's truly liberal democratic society, homosexuality, bisexuality, and transvestism are proudly taught to all schoolpersons as upstanding, wholesome lifestyles. Once a small percentage of the overall population, homosexuals now occupy over half the legislature, and it was one of the finest moments in our country's history when, only last year, we elected our very first transsexual president. Now every National Gayday celebration features long lines of self-flagellating, terribly repentant former heterosexuals, while our military divisions proudly mandate co-sexual bunks and showers, and many thriving businesses devote themselves wholly to the production of lingerie for pre-adolescent mascupersons. Our founding fatherpersons certainly would be no less proud than we.

The Renovated Constitution

Of all 437 Amendments to the Constitution, the earliest retain most value, for the integrity of the Amendments tend to resolve seemingly unrelated problems.

For instance, the Second Amendment worked in harmony with the First. Once the *right* to bear arms was firmly established, and virtually every American had become a walking armory, the Federal Government was successfully sued on the grounds that it most certainly *is* a guaranteed *right* of free speech to yell "Fire" in a crowded theater. Ps. Boris Q. de Little Feather courageously put this to the test by abruptly standing in a packed theater and yelling *"Fire!"* at the top of his lungs. Ps. de Little Feather's bullet-riddled body will forever be honored in the Heroes of Progressive Liberal Reform shrine in Allah Akbar State Park.

Compassion For The Masses

Arguably, the greatest breakthrough of Enlightened Liberal Reform came about with passage of the Victims' Relief Bill of 2077. What a glorious, emotion-packed day it must have been when those 170,000,000 Progressive Liberal Reformists linked arms across all 103 of the contiguous United States and chanted, *"Subsidization, Not Subjugation! Subsidization, Not Subjugation!"* until the very walls of the Rainbow House shook in the District of Vespuccia. And what an uplifting experience to be part of that gigantic assembly, tearfully escorting the hundreds of thousands of Aromatically Diverse and Morally Deprived unfortunates as they shuffled and jabbered into their tax-subsidized apartments to freely and democratically express themselves as Excretory Artists and Sensuality Scientists.

Freedom Of Expression

In closing I must again remark upon the stimulus for our awesome national pride. Only a truly liberal society such as ours would have the greatness to demand that every televised newscast crew include at least one Practicing Octogenarian Nudist, that every church sermon devote equal time to the oration of an atheist, and that every Intelligence Agency be made open to the General Public. It is *we*, the Progressive Liberals, who have exercised the vision to ensure that every major league team contain at least one paraplegic outfielder, that the Pentagon employ a fair quota of narcoleptics, and that, some rosy future day, the meek shall indeed inherit the earth.

Ps. Antoni-Levonitszchstein, I understand it is my legal obligation to inform you, prior to your grading this paper, that any mark below passing would compromise my sense of worthiness, and possibly result in a case of Student Afflicted by Misguided Educatory Officer Leading to Despair and Broken Self-esteem (SAMEOLDBS), a gross violation of my precious and hard-won Civil Rights. Please have your attorney contact mine if you have any questions.

"E.B." La Cszynevitch McGomez

PIETY

Old Malachi raced down the grade like the Devil was after him. Halfway to Piety he whirled and posed menacingly, all fang and fire, but the big staghound's glory days were history. He stood panting on trembling legs, his eyes glazing, and for a moment seemed hypnotized by the rising moon. In his imagination he snapped back at those pink staring eyes, reared at that gray hairy frame, bristled at that odd, not-quite human smell. Hacking ferociously, old Mal continued his skid in a flurry of tumbling pebbles and rising dust.

Abel's eyes popped open.

There it was again. All that racket could only be Job's squeamish hound. Still fully dressed against the cold, the boy hopped out of bed and threw open his window to another crystal clear West Virginia morning. Abel saw what appeared to be a pack of lanky ghosts moving dreamily up the pine-lined grade connecting Piety with the Shepherd's Mound valley overlook. The ghosts were lost in trees, reappeared writhing in moonlight, were lost again. The sound of hounds after prey was just beginning to carry when Malachi staggered into the settlement making enough noise to raise the dead. In seconds light was streaming from every window. Abel pulled on his heaviest coat and gloves, tiptoed downstairs, and gently disengaged his father's Winchester from above the mantel. He would have stepped outside but for a hairy hand on his shoulder.

Saul spun his son around, slowly unclenched his poised fist. He ran the hand up and down his face, gradually washing the fury from his expression. His eyes, still puffy with sleep, swept the faces gathering outside his door. "You maybe fixin on runnin off with the only rifle I got, boy?" He snatched the Winchester, grabbed the jamb and leaned out. *"Somebody shut that animal up!"* Malachi was heard gagging in a chokehold.

Saul would have reached for a lamp, but the full moon was tearing up the black morning sky. He studied his neighbors from the doorway's hollow, spat, and called, *"Boy!"* Abel's older brother limped through the crowd, fighting to keep tall.

"Dogs treed a bear, sir." Gabriel had to force his voice above a whisper. Saul's first-born lived in a ramshackle shed behind the house, out of view of healthy men and women. Piety's patriarch made certain, long ago, that the settlement's forty-odd residents were perfectly clear on genetics: blame for the young man's condition fell solely on the mother's side. Gabriel raised a deformed arm against the inferno in Saul's eyes; his father could whip his sons like dogs in public.

Saul swatted the arm away and shook the Winchester in Abel's face. "Next time you try that, boy, you'd best not let go so easy." He waited. *"Hear?"*

Abel looked away. "I hear you."

"Then, damn your eyes, *don't forget it!"*

As Saul tromped into the night the crowd immediately halved, leaving him plenty of room to stride. A muscle worked convulsively in Abel's jaw. He stepped outside with his heart in his fists.

Saul paused in a dirty pool of moonlight. He took his time filling and tamping a pipe, smoked thoughtfully for a while. There was very little eye contact. Aaron and Matthew, as always, were armed with family Bibles. Saul smiled back coldly, his nod almost imperceptible in the bowl's gentle flare. In this lull Gabriel slipped around the house and reappeared almost immediately, a pitchfork in one hand and a five-pound sledge in the other. He thrust the tines against Abel's chest. Abel snatched the handle and stared hard at his father's back.

Saul commenced a measured assault on the grade, flanked by his sons. Neighbors gathered in a loose trailing mob. The distant wailing of hounds was fading, but it was hard to tell whether they were receding in relation to the men or had been cut off by the pines. As the pace picked up, Saul cocked the Winchester and fired a single round. The hounds, recognizing the report, quieted immediately.

In less than a minute the first brown shape came whimpering downhill, quickly followed by four others. The dogs swam miserably around Saul while he tramped, snapping at one another and gnashing the air. No additional commands would be necessary.

That one blast dramatically increased the party's excitement. Men bunched into a hard driving line, their breaths puffing out like the steam plumes of racing locomotives. Saul pushed the pace harder still, the sides of his opened greatcoat swinging back and forth as he marched.

Something pale passed between the trees. The men and dogs swung around a stand of sage, and so came upon a bare patch of hillside. Now Abel was certain he saw a ghostly shape hurrying through a copse of immature pines. There was a reddish double flash as it turned back its head. The apparition vanished.

"*Git!*" Saul spat.

The hounds broke uphill and disappeared in the trees. A minute later the men stormed the copse and burst upon a rocky alcove nestled in pines. There the hounds had cornered their prey.

The body of men automatically fanned out in a crescent, sealing off the alcove. Although the hounds lunged ferociously, they were in no mood to attack. Whatever they'd pinned had them too confounded to leap.

It certainly wasn't a bear, though it was broad enough, and furry enough, to give that impression. The coat was a dull gray, covering everything except the mask, feet, and palms. Abel thought it behaved a lot like a man; in the way it stood upright without rearing, and in the way it swung its arms as it paced. But its hunched carriage and small head were absolutely unlike any human he'd encountered. As he watched the milling hounds he was reminded of the biblical Daniel, complacent in a den of lions.

Saul's impression couldn't have been more to the contrary. He was picturing himself as the central figure in a swirling display; a fearless superior in complete command. From this vantage he looked down on the scene, saw himself raise the rifle and draw a bead. When he cocked the Winchester the creature started. Every man expected it to rear or bolt, so there was complete surprise when it looked passively into Saul's face and meekly lowered its head.

Not a man imagined Saul had the guts to arbitrarily perform what amounted to an execution without provocation. But there he was, stepping forward deliberately, each pace marked by a blast from the Winchester.

Abel caught up before the echoes had died. "What'd you go and shoot it for, Pa?" He'd never seen such a coldhearted act.

"So help me, boy..." Saul lowered the rifle as the hounds bellied up, sniffing and crying oddly.

A voice in the crowd called, "Still kickin." Saul jabbed it twice, noting critically how it squirmed. Three shots had penetrated the chest, yet the escape of vital juices was mild.

Abel went down on one knee and sniffed. He closely studied the pink frothing mask. "What in the name of God *is* it?"

"Old Man," Gabriel whispered. "The Old Man of the Woods."

Saul's shook his head sardonically. "If my guess is any good it ain't nothin made in the name of God." He turned on the pressing bodies. "Now, you all get back. I *mean* it!" Curious white faces, moonlit crucifixes, brandished Bibles. Saul said with condescension, "Now, now, now—we all seen what we seen. This Thing creepin about. Good dogs actin like a bunch of women." He poked it with his rifle and snorted, "Name of God..."

"But it wasn't *doin* nothin!" Abel protested. "Didn't

come at us, didn't try to run."

Gabriel shook his head bravely. "You listen to Pa." He raised the sledge like a blacksmith and cocked his head. "You aim to finish it off, sir? Or you want me to?"

Saul cocked his head and draped a casual arm over the stunted boy's shoulders. "You run home, Gabe, and you fetch me a box of rail spikes, just the sharpest you can find."

"Sir?" Gabriel swallowed, looking from the prone Unknown to that familiar fire in his father's eyes. He dropped his head miserably and lowered the sledgehammer.

"Well, well," Saul cooed, "ain't we all sweet and soft now, little Gabriel? Just like your poor, disappointed Mommy would have wanted."

"Sir, I—"

"Do it!" Saul spat. "And don't you be tardy! I'm comin on mighty mean in my old age."

The Old Man thrashed wildly as the first spike ripped into flesh. Abel and Gabriel, clinging to handfuls of fur, would have been hurled aside if not for the quick support of half a dozen shouting men. The crowd swirled around the action hungrily, their moon-washed faces passing from bone-white to deep shadow—as Saul *again* raised the hammer, and *again* slammed it down. The final blow drove the spike solidly into wood. The Old Man whipped his head side to side and bowed his back. A shudder ran up his length.

When the crowd piled on he flailed hysterically. A fresh spike was driven through his left calf. The Old Man threw open his mouth in a long, wrenching shriek. The other leg was quickly impaled. He ceased screaming and froze in a wretched arch, favoring the wounded areas. The least move produced unbelievable agony.

Saul stood sweating, slowly clenching and unclenching his fingers, sucking saliva from the corners of his mouth. The primitive thrill passed from his eyes, and he relaxed.

"By God, sir," Gabriel managed, "that oughta—that *should* oughta show who's boss!"

"Look;" Abel whispered, as a series of spasms contorted the thing's pink, pug-like face, "it's still alive!"

Gabriel clamped a claw on Saul's hammer arm. "Needs a couple more whacks, sir, is all. Just a couple more."

Saul slowly turned his head. The full moon made Gabriel's face a ghastly mask of morbid excitement. Behind him, a dozen others displayed a gamut of expressions; from shock and revulsion to anticipation and bloodlust. By his quick and intuitive appraisal, Saul knew just where his support lay. He addressed those squeamish faces frostily, his heart brimming with contempt. "Lord," he said evenly, "I don't make no claim as to knowin everthin what goes on. I'm a simple man, and not above basic corruption. But I knows sin when I sees it, and I hereby grudge all them cowards what defies your bidding." He shook the hammer, flicked blood from his fingers. "God gimme the strength to do what's got to be done."

Saul draped his arms around his sons' shoulders. "Now I want you boys to stand this critter up in plain sight, so's everybody can see what I'm doin's right." He squeezed their arms affably, a kindly coach trying to drum up a little enthusiasm. "Somethin *special's* happenin here, boys! Somethin important! The Good Lord is testin us with this wicked monster— no other explanation possible." He gently steered them to the pine's rotted base and nudged the pitchfork with the toe of his boot. "Dig."

Saul relit his pipe and smoked patiently, facing the nervous crowd while Gabriel and Abel dug out a hole to post the pine. A nightmarish scream as his boys stood the tree upright, a round of moans from the neighbors. Saul smoked with affected nonchalance, for the first time in as long as he could remember battling a troubled conscience. It was that damned animal; wilting instead of defending itself, making him look bad in front of everybody. He turned back.

The thing's feet just touched the ground. A series of sobs escaped in irregular spurts, tapering to wet, hacking coughs. Gravity was pulling at the Old Man's length, stretching his wounds. Saul watched, fascinated. But as moonlight played over that flat twisted face, the cinched lids peeled apart and their opposing eyes locked. Saul shook from his widow's peak to his pinched, curling toes. Was this really *It*; that half-seen, scurrying creature of legend…sasquatch, troll, bogeyman, troglodyte; the fabled relic caught somewhere between man and subman…and would his god have created something so hideous and furtive, so *passive*? His words came back to haunt him— *was* this some sort of test? Just as blind ego was coming to his rescue, the thing's eyes rolled up and it renewed its moaning, but now with depth and continuity.

A hail of rocks battered the creature up and down. When the stoning ceased, Saul picked up Gabriel's hammer and a single spike. He guessed where the animal's heart should be. As he began his slow approach his doubt pursued him relentlessly. *Lord, give me courage. Guide my hand, guide my heart.*

Each new blow brought on a fresh convulsion, until the Old Man's frame crimped in a steady head-to-toe tremor. Eventually there could be no more pain. Nerves relaxed, violent contractions became feeble spasms.

The blows stopped.

Through a veil of blood the Old Man saw Saul step back, saw him grab a Bible from one man and a pitchfork from another. Saul weighed one against the other; the book in his left hand, the weapon in his right. He raised the pitchfork and held it high, hesitated.

The Old Man stared into eyes that glistened with an unfathomable rage. He stiffened and looked away, to where the tops of pines cut a jagged pattern in the false dawn, as Saul aimed the pitchfork for his throat, and with a grunt drove it home.

Just before sunrise Saul trudged back up the grade, bleary-eyed and uniquely troubled, the Winchester cradled loosely in his arm. Every time he'd begun to drift, the white cramp of conscience rocked him right back up. He needed to face his demon in the flesh, rather than have it stare back meekly in his imagination—and this time without the presence of all those skittish neighbors. More than this, he needed that mocking gray monster as a trophy, was fully prepared to tear it down and drag it back to Piety. With each boot's crunch he grew in confidence, and by the time he stormed round the copse he was his unshakeable old, jerky-tough self again.

Dogs, or some other big carnivores, had made quick work of the intruder, and now there wasn't much left; just a knot of gristly strands still fixed to the pine. The anticlimax was so unfair Saul froze right where he was, reduced to a minor observer in a very dim big picture. And, as he stood nonplussed, dawn's first ray burned down the hills, brilliantly lighting the scene. An unprecedented, overwhelming pang of shame dropped him to his knees.

For a while his mind was blank. Only gradually did he become aware of the stench of his sweat, of the crushing ache in his head, of the oddly sour taste of cold metal. With a most unmanly cry, Saul tore the Winchester's barrel from his mouth and dropped the rifle between his knees. He struggled to his feet. In the warming wash of sun Saul was a tempest of conflicting emotions, at war with himself as much as his environment. The pine's leaning shadow fell across his eyes. He looked up. Black with rage, Saul went ballistic on the affixed remnants; ripping the strands free with his nails, trying to tear out the spike using only his hands. When that failed, he grabbed the Winchester by the barrel and smashed the stock repeatedly against the spike, succeeding only in rocking it aside before shattering the stock completely. Saul collapsed with the effort, one arm clinging to the pine, the other dead at his side. When he again found his feet it was a bright new day. Saul pushed off and, embracing his chest, staggered back down the grade to break the news.

Lovers

Even as a child little Celia was obsessed with self-mutilation.

The first time April found her daughter semi-conscious and frothing, Celia's eyes were rolled back, her limbs and face lacerated by every sharp object within reach. Naturally mother went right into hysterics, and thereupon devoted all available time and energy into nursing her one love back to health. But the shock, to a hard woman perennially battling guilt and self-loathing, triggered something deeper than a healthy maternal reaction. From the moment she smashed that last bottle on the counter, April's response was anything but natural.

After Celia's recovery, mother and daughter lived in a home devoid of edges and points. April's small clapboard house, situated on a lonely tract of poorly-lit land, could be modified without the inquiries of authorities or neighbors. Panes were removed, windows boarded over. A carpenter was contracted to construct grilled apertures for light bulbs, and to fit all cupboards and drawers with miniature combination locks. Then April got busy. The resulting décor could best be described as *blunt,* as *fastidiously smooth,* and as *relentlessly contoured*, for April Winter, clad in overalls and bandanna, had methodically filed, sanded, and hammered flush every protrusion in her abusive ex-husband's seized home.

Yet there were additional gruesome episodes. April, focused only on that which openly met the critical eye, understandably ignored some pretty obvious potential hazards—simply because their projections were concealed by contours. Thus evils such as car keys and fountain pens were overlooked due to the *roundness* of their secreting handbag, and the oblong, peaked prongs protruding from the plugs of electric cords were neglected—not only because they were hidden in the parallel recesses of wall outlets, but because the plugs *themselves* were innocently smooth in appearance.

Now, April very deeply loved Celia. But there was a strong neurotic thread running through her affection, showing initially in a kind of overbearing *momminess*, and eventually in outright monomania. Because of this biochemical barrage, April blamed herself, unjustly, both for Celia's affliction and for the brutal alcoholic father's violent departure. Still, the woman was immensely strong, weathering Celia's desperate years of seizures and unforeseeable flesh savageries with uncommon courage and resolution. She grappled with depression by spending afternoons on the front porch, balancing pathos and palette while Celia slept locked away. During these imaginary sittings April painted her daughter in every setting she could concoct, with one proviso—the girl had to be smiling. April would have died to see just one of those painted smiles come alive. Her canvases were hung throughout the house, in obvious spots and in places marred by stubborn blood stains or bashed drywall.

These little hanging squares of artificial happiness became more important, and more strained, as Celia approached puberty. But April's pluck was amazing. For instance, during Celia's biting phase, mother had, after days of heroic soul-searching, resorted to having the girl's mouth wired shut, and still managed to abstain from gin and tonic until Celia discovered the exquisite tortures of manipulating stainless steel on freckled forearms and white, yearning wrists. Once the wires were removed, Celia became ferocious and unmanageable. It was with profound anxiety that April enlisted a most callous dental surgeon to, in strictest confidence, nearly dispatch the girl with anesthesia, that he might grimly extract her front uppers and lowers, leaving only those teeth adapted for grinding, rather than tearing. Little Celia, thus mutilated by another party, withdrew completely, and for a time immediately went into seizure at her mother's approach. The sweetly smiling portraits were now too upsetting for the toothless girl. Again showing her mettle, April overcame her horror daily as she painted out teeth, canvas by canvas, solely for her disturbed daughter's sake.

Alcoholism is such an ugly, such a harsh and unforgiving word. Yet in April's case it was tantamount to emotional salvation. Through regular and liberal self-medication, she was able to remain all-giving mother first, self-indulgent masochist second. Strange that strength and weakness should cohabit with such balance. April throve on stresses that would crush a less-adamant individual...even during those many long drunken nights with her ex, before he'd blacked her eyes and sent her gushing and convulsing to the emergency room, she had indulged in a form of liquor abuse-gratification common to women of low self-esteem: *The bastard beat her. He ripped her off, he raped her. He used her in ways that are incomprehensible to even the shallowest student of ethics.* But...damn it, at least he was *there.*

April fought down these horrors courageously, so that now the past was just a binge; one long, perilously survived stupor. The present was all that mattered. And the present was Celia. For April, loving Celia was the purest form of giving, because Celia didn't—Celia couldn't—*take.* And even a masochist is sobered by rejection.

As to the growing girl's security, April was inflexible. She would not admit visitors, *period*, unless they obeyed a single rule: at no time, under any circumstances, was a sharp object permitted indoors. Pockets were ordered emptied, with heartfelt apologies. Purses and suspicious personal articles were kept outside in a locked strongbox secured to the porch, and only then was adolescent Celia allowed to mingle with her mother's genuinely supportive and sympathetic friends. For a time this method afforded April the semblance of a social life. Then, one Sunday morning, a fellow hospital receptionist unintentionally left behind a simple straight pin that had been lodged in the hidden seam of her recently altered pantsuit. The physical consequences of that single pin were devastating. April entertained no longer; she became a psychological as well as a physical recluse, and changed her work schedule to the graveyard shift to be near Celia during the teenager's waking hours.

It was on this shift that she met Will, an easygoing security guard with an inexhaustible patter. In the wee hours, when it seemed they were the only creatures alive, the two would sit in the hard fluorescent light and chat, and flirt, and the dreary hours would not seem so long. They shared a love of pasta, a lifelong passion for jazz, and a real fondness for stargazing. And they had something else in common. One black morning, during April's lunch break, Will came by to point out M31 in Andromeda. While so doing he nonchalantly draped his other arm over her shoulders, reached inside his fur-lined jacket, and slid forth a nearly full pint of Cream of Kentucky bourbon.

After that their working lives were inextricably entwined. They came to the hospital eagerly, and stole away at every opportunity. April now brought her gin and tonic in a plastic thermos, while Will carried a holstered flask of bourbon under his security bomber jacket. They weren't stupid. They were never recklessly drunk, and they were never caught. Week by week the consummation of their passion neared.

The effect of alcohol on Will was to rouse an irrepressible satyr; a beast diametrically opposed to the sober, affable security guard April had fallen for. He couldn't keep his hands off her; any excuse and no excuse were reasons enough to justify a grope here, a pinch there. For her part, April found it increasingly difficult to maintain her half-hearted parries. It had been so long. She giggled and blushed at his touch, and their façade of professionalism gradually crumbled, to the whispered amusement of janitors and orderlies. Alone together, they tore at their drinks.

One peaceful Saturday night there was an unexpected knock on April's door. In the bulb's sallow haze a half-tanked Will stood hunched like a punch-drunk fighter, his primer-gray pickup parked with one wheel on the curb. April hesitated; everything was wrong. This eager event should be taking place at a motel, on a back seat, in the park—anywhere but here. But Will hadn't come to be turned away, and April was still prey to the alcoholic cycle: just the sight of Will drunk and weaving triggered an almost Pavlovian reaction. She experienced a kind of contact high, and her suddenly surging libido just as suddenly *demanded* she fix herself a drink. This she did, in nervous spurts, while talking to Will through the door; telling him to keep his voice down, asking him to be patient. She threw on a favorite album and gulped down half her drink. The liquor warmed her blood, the music took her mood. Excited, alive again, she peeked into the black womb of her daughter's room. Celia was in her familiar sleeping posture; curled into a fetal position, eyelids fluttering, the orbs rolled back. April tiptoed in, readjusted the covers. Tiptoed out. Gently locked the door.

Will knew all about Celia from their chats at work. So, drunk though he was, he *behaved*; he was expectant, but compliant. He docilely placed his keys and all other loose objects in the strongbox, then proudly displayed the tall unbreakable Tupperware flask that held his liquor. April was brutally thorough in her physical search, much to Will's delight, and at long last, after snapping shut the combination lock on the box, she ushered him inside.

Only April's greater sobriety enabled her to keep Will at bay. For a while the man seemed indefatigable in his advances, but finally the bourbon began to work against him. He sagged, and allowed her to ease him onto the couch. April sauntered into the kitchen, returning a minute later with paper cups, a teak bowl full of ice, and a plastic pitcher filled with gin and tonic water. In the space of that minute Will had recovered completely, and was randy as ever. Their embrace was immediate. Will hauled her down on the couch, his greedy hands fumbling with her blouse and bra, his breath hot in her ear. Suffocating, April pushed him off, and they both leaned on the sanded-round coffee table with the sanded-round feet, gulping their drinks out of sheer nervousness.

She tried to forestall the inevitable—with chatter, with counter-maneuvers—but Will only grew bolder, scattering pillows and spilling drinks. April, capitalizing on the break, squirmed out of his embrace and made to replenish the pitcher. Will wobbled to his feet and blocked her way meaningfully. For half a minute April was terrified, but Will only grinned, stole a kiss, and staggered off to the bathroom. By the time he'd returned, April had wolfed down a stiff drink and forgotten both the pitcher and her anxiety. The two fell on the couch as the music's final strains were replaced by the rhythmic *hiss-ca-chuk* of the record player's stylus at the label's paper perimeter. Behind this rhythm came a familiar scratch and rattle.

Celia's door cracked open. The girl peeked out timidly.

In a heartbeat April was wholly mother again. She shoved Will away, swayed to her feet, and held out her arms while Celia shuffled over shyly, confused and vulnerable in her floral-print pajamas. The conflicting emotions could produce only one response: April quickly broke the mother-daughter embrace and made for the kitchen and gin.

Celia was fascinated by Will; tugging at his clothes and hair while he glared. He sullenly pulled at his drink, his expression continuing to darken as April stumbled back to the couch, a fresh bowl of ice quaking in her hand. She must have blacked out for a minute, must have tumbled backward onto the couch, for the next thing she knew Will was straddling her with his face buried in her chest. He pinned her like a butterfly. April whipped her head side to side in protest, and Will went right out of his mind with passion. When her head came to rest she was looking straight into Celia's bright and wondering eyes. April cried out and tried to pull free, only inflaming Will further. He threw all his weight on her, and, so great was his demand, would probably have taken her then and there if not for a haymaker to the tip of his nose. April struggled to her feet and stood reeling in the middle of the room. Will blinked at her stupidly, his right hand gripping her rent and rumpled blouse. His other hand rose slowly, the fingers testing his hot bleeding nose. His eyes darkened.

April retained only vague impressions of the ensuing few minutes. She remembered watching Will lurch to his feet and trip headlong over the coffee table, waving his arms like a drowning man. She recalled seeing him hit the floor in a hail of scattered ice, oscillate and bob to his knees, flail and lurch to his feet.

In slow motion Will lunged, grabbed April by the hair with his left hand, hauled back his right arm, and smashed his fist flush in her face.

The blow sent April backpedaling into the kitchen. She glanced off a cabinet, slammed against the refrigerator, slid to the floor. Through a veil of blood she watched Will stumbling back and forth in the doorway, moving like a ping pong ball jamb to jamb, sinking gradually, at last turning on Celia and dragging her kicking and screaming to the floor. Shrieking right along, April somehow pushed herself to her hands and knees; but that was all she could manage before the combined effects of nearly a fifth of gin and a broken nose sent her reeling into pitch.

April's eyes opened around four in the morning. She rolled onto her stomach, crawled a few feet, and was violently sick. Except for a narrow wedge of bare perceptibility created by streaming moonlight, the house was inky dark—and that one realization was so powerful it overwhelmed all April's physical ills combined: *the front door was ajar.* Overturned shapes projected dimly in the living room. April, fighting for air, ricocheted off those shapes to the doorway, steadied, thrust out her caked, swollen face.

Will lay spread-eagled on the lawn; face-down and unconscious. His truck's passenger door hung open, its wing window smashed. A number of smallish, dully shining objects were scattered about the lawn, leading in a winding trail from Will's body to the porch. A few of these articles showed far away, as though violently tossed.

April's puffy eyes followed the trail back to the porch. At her feet a wide, flat toolbox lay upturned amidst a number of screwdrivers, spanners, and miscellaneous small parts. Chisels and a hammer lay atop the bashed and battered strongbox—the combination lock had been scored and defaced in a fit of drunken rage. She shook from head to toe. Screwdrivers. Chisels.

April turned back and the room turned right along with her. It kept on turning while she felt her way through the darkness, barking her shins on the jumbled unseen. The black maze became too much. Still drunk out of her mind, she pitched onto her face, striking her chin hard on the naked wood floor. Inches from her eyes, a number of half-melted ice cubes gleamed whitely. But it seemed odd, even in her muddled state, that the cubes hadn't fully melted. April's eyes burned with the strain. Unwilling to believe her heart over her mind, she picked up a cube and rolled it between her forefinger and thumb. It was cold, certainly, and slippery, but April *knew*, without the benefit of direct light, that she was holding one of Celia's bloody severed toes. In a dream she pushed herself to her feet and fell against her daughter's door, kicked it open, fumbled for the light switch.

Celia was seated on the floor with her back propped against the bed. Between her splayed legs lay several articles from Will's tool box, including a small hatchet, a large awl, and a heavy-duty *exacto knife*. The girl had chopped off her toes and fingertips with the hatchet, torn her limbs and torso to ribbons with the blade, and used the awl to make mushy pools of her eyes. Only her mouth was untouched. The same toothless grin that dominated a hundred wall portraits now smiled up at a failed mother in an alcoholic haze. Completely undone, April fell screaming on the little corpse of her love.

Thelma

Behind every shop window lies a strange and magical world; a world where half-defined shapes, busily engaged in mysterious transactions, seem to coalesce even as they pass from view. These unstable figures—customer, employee, and proprietor—are *important* people. They are not there to be rudely eyeballed, like so many fish in a bowl. Their business is theirs and theirs alone.

But old Thelma couldn't help staring, no matter how hard she tried, no matter how many times she was punished. Her head would be turning before she knew it, and sometimes, squinting against the mirrored sun, she would catch one or more of those murky shop-dwellers staring back importantly just as her hunched and gnarled reflection rolled by.

Thelma was crazy about people. Whether they pointed and whispered, or rudely laughed out loud, she always smiled in their eyes, resisting with difficulty the urge to reach out and touch. And she loved bustle. People walked this way and that, jealously guarding their personal space, but they invariably parted when she rolled down the sidewalk, as if she were a queen being escorted through a sea of loving subjects.

The sidewalks were bustling now, and Thelma could barely contain her excitement. He eyes devoured everything. When her chair finally came to a rest she found herself staring at a small box affixed to a pole. She'd seen this kind of fixture hundreds of times, and was mesmerized by the experience. The fixture poked out right at eye level, and bore a flat white plate with a wonderful little cryptogram of a funny black stick man hovering over a long black arrow. The stick man gave the impression of being in an awful hurry to discover the big secret that long black arrow was about to divulge. For some reason these fixtures always featured a blunt metal button beneath the cryptogram.

Perhaps it was the fascinating way people now all burst off the curb as one. Or maybe it was the intoxicating combination of crisp air and golden sun. But suddenly Thelma just had to solve the mystery, just had to push that stubby little button.

A hand whacked her across the back of her head; not hard enough to really hurt, just hard enough to let her know she'd done wrong. Right behind the sound of the whack came Gary's voice:

"God *damn* you, you ugly old witch. How many times do I have to tell you to keep your fucking paws on the armrests?" The hand grabbed the white bun of her hair and twisted back her head. Gary's eyes were burning. "The next fucking time you try that, retard, you're gonna go to bed without dinner. You got me? You remember what it's like going to bed without dinner? You cried like a baby all night, didn't you? Well, that's what you get when you fuck up, y'hear? So don't press your luck." He pushed her head back down, but not too hard. There were pedestrians everywhere.

Thelma craned her neck to look back remorsefully. "Pleezh no be madda me, Gehr. I be good."

Gary exhaled noisily. "My ass." He shoved the wheelchair across the intersection and rammed it against the curb, then kicked, shook, jerked, and heaved it onto the sidewalk, swearing up and down. But his demeanor changed abruptly as another old biddy, the widow Bender, approached and came to a halt directly in their path.

"Widow Bender! And how are you on this lovely fall day?"

"In the pink," the widow lied. She stooped to smile in Thelma's face. "Hi, Thelma dear! So…I see you and your nice young man are out enjoying the day. How's he been treating you? Just like the princess you are, I'll wager."

"Oh yesh," Thelma gushed. "Gehr gooda me. Gehr always gooda Telma."

"That…that's wonderful!" the widow grimaced. "I—" she managed, "I've got to *go* now, dear," for in her passion Thelma had allowed her arthritic old talon to grasp one of the widow's hands. The widow extracted her hand with difficulty, smiled breezily at Gary and winked. "Well, you just make sure you give him a big long kiss for me, sweetheart." She looked back down. "Bye now, Thelma!"

"That was rich," Gary said as they continued down the sidewalk. He snickered. "'Gehr always gooda Telma'. You bet your ass I'm good to you, crone. Who else would put up with your goddamned babytalk bullshit. Who else would have the balls to tolerate your shithole stench all fucking day long. You gnarly pig. You don't know—you couldn't possibly imagine— how many times I've dreamed of just walking off and leaving you and your stupid-ass chair in rush hour traffic."

Thelma looked back fearfully. "Oh no, Gehr! Pleezh no leave me, Gehr. Telma be good."

"Oh-h-h—you don't gotta worry about me leaving you, witch. I'll be pushing your spastic ass around until the day you die. And you wanna know why? I'll tell you why. Because you're worth a hell of a lot more alive than dead, that's why. The state pays good money to keep corpses like you going, and a nice piece of that pie goes into my pocket for taking care of you." He laughed harshly. "I'm your fucking guardian, you ugly old asshole; I'm your goddamn guardian angel. I'm the one who feeds you and medicates you and makes sure you don't slobber to death. You didn't know that, did you—that I'm as close to God as you'll ever get, that I'm the one who's responsible for keeping your stinking ass in one piece? Even though I've told you a thousand times…you don't know *shit*, do you dimwit? So I'll be around forever, even though you're, what, a hundred and fifty years old? Even though you're ugly as sin and smell like the dead...wait a minute! What am I saying? *Like* the dead? You *are* dead. You're just a rotting old cadaver that some trick of fate keeps running. And you know *what*, you funky old skank? You'll outlive us all! Great people, *important* people, will pass out of the picture naturally. But not stupid stinking Thelma. She'll just hang in there, baby. Pissing and whining and waiting for good old Gary to do *everything* for her. Cunt! You're dirt, that's all you are. Just plain dirt."

"I do betta, Gehr," old Thelma moaned, despising herself. "I sho sharry, Gehr. I be betta, I promiss. Telma be good fum now on, Gehr. Telma be good."

Her apology was lost on Gary. He leaned forward to whisper in her ear, "And you wanna know *why* you don't deserve to be alive? Because you're worthless, y'hear? *Worthless!* You're not good for anything or anybody. You can't take care of yourself, you can't feed yourself, you can't do squat. When's the last time you did anything constructive, or had even one original thought? When's the last time you made the slightest effort to be of value to anything? I'll tell you when: *never!* 'Cause you're a sick old piece of shit who can't see past her goddamn wheelchair. A cockroach has more value than you. At least a fucking cockroach can get around on its own."

Gary shoved and jerked the wheelchair to make his point. "Don't you understand, shitbrain? Life is *good* to you. But what good are you to life? Where on this fucking planet is there a single life-form, not counting Yours Truly, that benefits from your being here. Name one thing. Can't do it, moron? That's because you're *worthless!* But I'll clue you in on something. When the golden day arrives that your filthy ass expires, tramp, you're gonna make a whole lot of worms real happy. Party time for Ourobouros. *That's* when you're gonna contribute."

Gary abruptly turned the wheelchair to the left, steered it across the street and into the park. "Aw-w-w..." he concluded, "what's the use."

This was Thelma's favorite part of the day. Everyone in the park was always so happy, so full of vitality. Children squealed with delight, dogs chased Frisbees, lovers drifted langorously between the elms. And around them all bumped the slowly rolling chair, pushed by the mumbling and incongruously sullen man, his head down.

"*Jesus*, here we go again! Everybody and his mother out having the time of their lives. Every guy in town but me walking along with a hot young babe on his arm. Look what I'm stuck with. Oh man, am I embarrassed! You dumb lump of shit. I'm the laughingstock of this neighborhood thanks to you."

Gary's mood continued to deteriorate, in stark contrast to the afternoon's waking loveliness. After wheeling her twice through the park he brought her chair to a halt next to a trash bin.

"Okay, Quasimodo. Have a last look around. I'm gonna go take a leak and be right back." He stuck a forefinger in her face. "Now don't you move! I'm warning you. You stay put just where you are. Don't you dare talk to anybody and don't you dare touch anything. I'll be right back." He gave her a hard look and ambled over to a public restroom.

Thelma sat stock-still, determined to be good. But her mind was rocking back and forth, chanting: *Don't be bad, Thelma; don't make Gary mad. Don't be bad, Thelma, don't be bad!* This little mantra went round and round in her head until it ceased to make sense.

Thelma heard a rustling near her feet, but fought the impulse to look. Gary had told her not to move. If she could only once do what he said maybe he wouldn't be so unhappy all the time. Again came the rustling, followed by a tiny, frightened mewing. Thelma's hands gripped the armrests. The mewing grew in urgency until Thelma could no longer resist the temptation to peek.

The tiny white kitten couldn't have been more than three or four weeks old. It had one brown ear and a large brown spot on its forehead. It was obviously abandoned and extremely hungry.

Thelma fell in love with it right away. Her rheumy old eyes went teary, and her wretched old hand reached down to caress it. The kitten recoiled at her touch, then rubbed against her thumb. Every cell in Thelma's body trembled. "Ghity," she said.

Gary now walked back, looking bored. "Okay, fuckface. Time to wheel your stupid ass home and—*hey!* What you got there?"

Thelma looked up at Gary's frowning face. Her cheeks were covered with tears. "Ghity," she bubbled.

Gary grimaced. "Leave it alone, damn you! What do you want with a fucking cat, anyway? Don't I feed you enough? No! Out of the question." He looked around, picked up a wood slat and swatted at the kitten, trying to scare it away. All he got for his effort was a sizable splinter in his index finger. Gary howled as if he'd been gored, swore and dashed over to a drinking fountain to wash off the wound. In less than a minute he was back, but not before Thelma had managed to reach down, grab the kitten, and bundle it under her sweater.

"Shit!" Gary spat. "Look what you fucking caused, whore. Oh, *mama*, that hurts! I oughta knock your fucking head off, you know that, you old bitch? You're good and goddamned lucky I need you alive."

Thelma withered under Gary's invective as he wheeled her home, occasionally bashing the chair against walls, pushing it hard off curbs. She had been bad again, but it didn't seem to matter. All that mattered was the tender little source of warmth shifting position on her lap. Each small movement jangled her nerves. Under her sweater she gently stroked the tiny creature. The warmth hummed in response. "Ghity," she whispered.

Gary unlocked and kicked open the front door in one move. He shoved Thelma's chair in roughly. "Jesus, bitch, don't fight me! You know the fucking routine. Sit still!" He kicked the door closed, heaved a sigh. After a moment he wordlessly pushed the chair to the ramp and up to the converted attic. The attic had been partitioned centrally to create a sunroom on one side and a small bedroom on the other. This was Thelma's room. "Here you are, fossil: back in your digs. Enjoy. I'll be downstairs in the real world. Do me a favor. If you need anything, call the undertaker. Stay out of my face." He turned and walked down the stairs abutting the ramp.

Thelma waited until she heard the familiar sound of the television downstairs, then carefully opened her sweater to reveal the kitten's tiny crimped form. The poor thing was trembling in its sleep, and barely responded when Thelma tenderly cradled it in her arms. The old woman and kitten trembled together as the afternoon sun burnished the bedroom's bare wood floor.

"Ghity," Thelma crooned, rocking slowly in her chair. "Ghity, ghity, baby ghity."

Now sunshine began to play upon a corner of the small card table that served as Thelma's desk and dining table. She wheeled over and very gently lifted the kitten onto the warm spot. It wakened and struggled to stand while she supported it with one hand under its belly. Once it was upright it began to urgently rub its cheeks against her other hand, then attempted to suckle a finger. It was starving. Old Thelma kissed it, over and over. It was all she could do.

Without any warning Gary came barging into the room. When he saw the kitten on the table he stopped dead in his tracks. His mouth fell open as he stared from Thelma to the kitten and back again. Finally he breathed, "You *bitch!* What did I tell you? *What did I tell you?"* He took a great step forward and slapped Thelma hard across the face. "I told you 'no fucking cat', didn't I? *Didn't I tell you that?"* He scooped the kitten in his hand, stepped to the window, and screamed. "DIDN'T I TELL YOU NO FUCKING CAT?" Staring hard at her, he threw the kitten out the window as if it was so much garbage. Thelma hugged herself, horrified. Gary stormed over and grabbed her by the hair, began slapping her face back and forth, his passion ascending with each consecutive blow. Finally he caught himself, almost hysterical, but still together enough to realize the stupidest thing he could do would be to leave marks. He stepped back.

"You've crossed me for the last time, cocksucker." He tore her mirror from the wall, smashed it on the floor. He pointed a shaking finger at the shards of glass. "You see that?" he spat, indicating a piece. "That's you." He jabbed his finger at other pieces. "You see that? You see that? You see that? That's what's gonna happen to you next time you disobey me." He knocked a picture off the wall, moved to the closet and tore Thelma's clothes from their hangers. Then his anger seemed to abate.

He walked to the door and said coldly, almost calmly, "No more privileges. Period. No more trips to the park, no more listening to the radio. This door stays locked, and you stay in." He appeared about to elaborate, but his anger was catching up with him again. Finally he stepped out, screamed, *"Fuck you!"* and slammed the door so hard it shook the walls.

The aftermath was worse than the explosion. Thelma sat in shock, wondering only how she could have been so bad. She wiped away her tears with a deformed and quivering hand. This was the unhappiest she'd ever made Gary, and the first time he'd ever locked her away from him. An exaggerated sense of lonesomeness weighed upon her. She loathed herself. Gary was right. She didn't deserve to live.

Little by little the numbness grew over her. Her thoughts slunk farther from meaningful analysis, and an almost palpable silence enveloped the room. It was in this oppressive silence that she thought she heard a familiar sound.

Thelma's attention refocused, her heart began to pound. There it was again. A tiny sound, frightened and lost, seeming to come from right outside the window. Entranced, old Thelma rolled her chair over.

She leaned out. The white kitten lay straddled over the rain gutter running above the eaves and just under her window, having hit a power line and fallen to its present position. If not for the line the animal, small as it was, would certainly have been killed or seriously injured by an impact with the cement drive below.

Thelma's brows ran oblique. The kitten perched awkwardly on one of the wide steel clamps securing the rain gutter to the roof, a good seven or eight feet from the window's trim. Thelma gripped the rain gutter, tried to shake it to get the kitten's attention. The gutter was solidly attached and didn't budge at all, but the kitten must have felt the vibrations, for it looked up and wailed pitifully.

"Ghity!" Thelma moaned. She rolled her chair back from the window, trying to think. But she had precious little experience in problem solving. The harder she thought the more confused she became. She must have nodded, must have dozed for an hour or more. The next thing she knew it was getting chilly, and there was the sound of a key in the lock.

Gary came in with a small blue plastic bowl in one hand and a plastic drinking glass half-full of water in the other.

"Here's your gruel, ghoul." He placed the bowl and glass on the card table. "That's right. All you get is formula. No meat, no vegetables, no sweets. It serves your stupid ass right for being such a sneaky old slut. And that's *all* you're gonna get from now on, until I think you've learned your lesson." His face twisted with contempt. "You mangy whore. I'm being way too kind for the likes of you. If I had my druthers you'd starve to death up here. Oh, yeah! I'd crank up the T.V. and you could scream your ugly old head off for all I'd care." He crashed his fist on the dresser, then swept off Thelma's little ceramic menagerie. "But I need you *alive*, pigface!" He took a deep breath. "There's enough nutrition in that slime to keep you going. But that's all. We'll see how tough you are after a few days of goop diet." He turned and walked to the door. Before he slammed it he said icily, "You'll live. But so help me, bitch, I'll live to piss on your grave."

Thelma waited a minute, then pushed herself over to the card table. She inspected the contents of the bowl. "Formula" was a vitamin-rich concoction mass-produced for the elderly, but lately Gary had been saving pennies by preparing his own version; basically a blend of milk, margarine, and sugar.

Thelma anxiously looked around the pigsty of her room. There was trash and filth everywhere. Not only had Gary never once lifted a finger to clean the room, he seemed to take a vicious delight in haphazardly storing junk more properly assigned to the garage or basement.

Now Thelma rooted through a pile next to her bed, looking for something that would extend her reach. After an exhaustive search she settled on a grimy aluminum curtain hanger. It was the retracting kind: two nearly identical lightweight rods that fit one into the other for sliding adjustment. One end of each rod was crooked at a right angle for securing the device to a wall. Thelma found that by forcing the assembled hanger to its greatest length she had a good six feet of extension for her arm.

She had to rest. This had been a tremendous amount of effort for a crippled and sedentary nonagenarian. She was beginning to doze when the kitten's mewing renewed its tug on her heart. Thelma continued her rooting, fished out a heavy rubber band. The band was an inch and a half wide, perhaps twice that in circumference. It was difficult to stretch.

Thelma wheeled back to the card table and placed these items before her. She was breathing hard. After a minute she drank the water from the plastic glass. The room seemed to revolve, steadied. Thelma forced the rubber band around the base of the glass, then moved it upward an inch at a time. The pressure of the band cracked the plastic in three places. Puffing and wheezing, old Thelma now pushed one end of the curtain hanger under the rubber band until the two parts were secure, making a six-foot-long handle for the glass. Outside, the kitten began to cry continuously.

Thelma lifted the bowl of formula and held it over the glass. Her hands were shaking so badly that this job—the simple act of pouring the contents of one vessel into another—was accomplished only with the greatest difficulty. A good deal of formula oozed out the cracks in the glass. Thelma wiped the bowl clean with her crooked old finger, then smeared this residue around the rim of the glass. She balanced her little device on the wheelchair's armrests and rolled to the window.

Thelma thrust out her head. The white kitten was still straddling the clamp over the rain gutter. When it saw her it began to wail and move its legs ineffectually.

"No, ghity, no," Thelma cooed. "Ghity stay." She maneuvered her contraption out the window so that the base of the glass rested on the floor of the rain gutter, then began to push it slowly toward the kitten. A lot of formula was lost in the process.

All this activity was hard on the old woman, and by the time the glass had reached the kitten Thelma's arms were shaking. Very little formula remained in the glass, but the kitten attacked the nourishment ravenously, licking the inside of the glass clean and lapping up the inch of liquid on the bottom. With the last of her strength, Thelma dragged the device back inside and let her head fall on the sill.

The kitten was still hanging on the clamp, still straining to lap up the spilled drops.

Thelma watched it listlessly, unable to lift her head. An absolutely novel feeling began to grow in the old woman's heart; a sense of worthiness, of responsibility. Something small and vulnerable...something *unimportant*—but something very much alive—depended on *her*. Life desperately needed her, contemptible as she surely was, and Thelma found herself weeping uncontrollably while her heavy head lolled on the sill and the afternoon sun gently washed her face.

The next day Thelma slept very late. When at last she rose she became dizzy and weak from the act of sitting upright. The normal procedure of working her misshapen body into the wheelchair was an almost Herculean task.

She struggled over to the window. The kitten was sprawled exactly as she'd seen it last, and her heart skipped a beat. She passionately shook the rain gutter. When the animal finally lifted its head and sluggishly cried out she was so relieved she had to cling to the sill.

All day long she remained at the window, talking as much to herself as to the kitten, her mind slipping in and out of reality.

Gary came in late in the day. He glared and refused to say a word, plopped down the bowl of formula and glass of water. He scowled and slowly shook his head. Thelma was too weak to acknowledge him, so he walked back out and locked the door.

After a few minutes Thelma retrieved her device from under the bed, patiently slopped formula from bowl to glass, forced her chair to the window.

As soon as the glass reached the kitten it came to life. It attacked the mixture eagerly, lapping up even those drops trapped in the cracks. Old Thelma was so exhausted she fell asleep with her head and arms out the window, and didn't wake until it was fully dark and quite chilly. It took a supreme effort to make it back to bed.

That night she came to her senses alternately shivering and sweating. Her room seemed unfamiliar. Thelma pulled a heavy sweater over her flimsy nightdress, covered herself snugly, and let herself drift.

On the third day she remained in bed, her hands and feet freezing. Gary waited until near sunset to bring in her formula. Thelma feigned sleep to avoid him, then woozily fought her way through the steps of boarding her wheelchair, filling the glass, making her way to the window.

The kitten cried frantically when it saw her. Thelma pushed the glass, which seemed a dead weight, to where the kitten could just reach it. Her arms began to shake terribly, but she managed to keep the glass in place until the kitten had finished.

All sensation passed from her left arm.

Thelma gasped. Her upper body jerked. The glass and curtain hanger flipped over the rain gutter and dropped into a hedge below the window.

Thelma's hand reflexively pushed her away from the window, the wheelchair rolling her back a few feet. There she sat quietly, wondering at the lack of feeling in the arm. It might have been made of wood. She lifted the wooden arm with her good hand, placed the arm neatly on its rest, then used the good hand to push those rigid fingers one by one into a semblance of grip.

She watched the day expire, saw the full splendor of its passing face for the final time, while shadows crept along the walls and floor, steadily dabbing up random pools of light.

The sky caught fire. Within the window's frame stray plumes ignited, slowly lost their intensity and glory, then smoldered with a dull and bloody glow. As the fire subsided these plumes turned to smoke in the deepening blue, became vagabond ghosts in the dark, lost their way in the night, and were no more.

Death treads gently on gentle souls.

The end came for Thelma not with abruptness or horror, nor did it bring her any pain. It mirrored twilight's subtle diminuendo; measure by measure muting voice, shading tone.

It was almost an elegant thing.

Night stepped through the window not as a burglar but as a suitor, drawing its endless shroud about her, round and round, claiming her pulse one revolution per beat. It worked its way up her arms, her neck, her face.

Thelma watched the stars writhe prettily above the horizon, burning out their hearts for no one and nothing. She watched them shimmer, languidly, until a breath of cold blew out the light in her eyes.

In the wee hours there came a tiny scuffling at the window. A brown ear appeared, then a white ear, and finally two round eyes peered liquidly into the room. The kitten mewed nervously for a few seconds, then half-jumped, half-fell to the floor.

It froze where it landed, questing with its senses. In a minute it squinched and crept to where the two orthopedic shoes stood on the footrest. It climbed awkwardly over the rest and onto a shoe. There it paused to look up uncertainly. It clawed with difficulty up Thelma's leg and thence onto her lap. The old woman was cold as stone. The little white kitten threw back its head and wailed. It cried on and on and on in the darkness, rocking side to side, rhythmically digging its claws left and right into her cheap cotton nightdress. When it stopped, the room was quiet as a tomb. Slowly the kitten pushed its way under her sweater until it was all but buried. It curled up tightly, began to hum. It closed its eyes and was almost immediately asleep.

Shade

Even at this, the final hour of my overlong and entirely miserable life, I can distinctly recall the first time I encountered the apparition…the stranger—what shall I call it—the *thing* that has haunted my every waking hour of this one dogged existence, and taken full possession of even those few hours per day I ruefully describe as sleep.

I must have been, I think, five or six years old when the first intruder appeared, approaching calmly as I sat by the little whitewashed picket fence girding our home's buttercup-bordered front lawn. I remember him as a man of perfectly ordinary appearance; that is to say there was nothing singularly remarkable about his countenance or carriage. But he came sauntering up to me then, running his hand casually over the dull white points of the pickets as he made his way along the sidewalk, and, in the most straightforward and intimate of tones, hailed me by name. I was too young to do anything but gape with complete innocence, expecting to see a neighbor, or to recognize one of my father's many successful friends. But the looming figure was unknown to me, although his words and demeanor indicated a relationship both close and (odd from the perspective of a child) *enduring*. And this man told me, quite pleasantly, that he'd been keeping a very close eye on me, and would be maintaining his surveillance. So saying, he smiled, nodded, and continued on his way. Startled, yet still too ingenuous to know any impulse more complex than wonder, I at length gained my feet and peered shyly round the gatepost. And I can still remember watching him strolling down the walk, admiring the azaleas and rhododendrons, all the way to the little market on the corner, where I lost sight of him in the shadow of a billboard. I never saw the man again.

This, I say, was only the first encounter with the macabre fear that has never ceased to pursue me. My parents, outside of encouraging my unease with strict admonitions about not talking to strangers, provided no enlightenment whatsoever as to the amiable man's design. So I commenced performing, as frightened children will, unnecessary searches of closets, the space beneath my bed, and other likely hiding places, but with a most uncommon zeal. No bogeymen were to be found. Yet it was through the persistence of these searches that I eventually found myself paying closer attention to areas *naturally darker* than their surroundings. And one July afternoon, while for the thousandth time surveying an alcove of dense shade created by the convergence of tall hedges and a handsome sycamore in our expansive back yard, I began to entertain a most unsettling notion of being...watched. I stood there paralyzed, or rather I should say hypnotized, for the better part of half an hour, sweating freely in the hot summer sun, yet far too timid to seek comfort. And such is the power of the human imagination that my eyes, steadfast and unblinking, in time began to perceive a kind of form where no form existed. My mind *sculpted* a presence out of nothingness. And I saw, or fancied I saw, what appeared to be two dull orbs suspended some six feet off the ground. From these imagined specters it was easy to induce what could only be a pair of eyes. And my fancy, fueled now by a very real fear, continued to extrapolate—I seemed to perceive pupils in those orbs, and, at last, a kind of contour, or *mantle*, that surrounded the vision. When I finally lost all courage and slunk away, I was absolutely convinced that those "eyes" followed my every move. And yet the most arresting particular of this experience, and therefore the most memorable, was not the actual instance of those imagined eyes, but something unfathomable in their aspect. To this day I have endeavored to find word or words which will aptly convey their overwhelmingly morbid, inflexible, bruised-yet-bloodless expression. No such word or words will relieve me. No such model exists.

The next visitation occurred upon my entering junior high school, at that tender age when peer pressure impresses itself so adamantly upon the psyche. This time the intruder was a youngster of my own age, and of generally similar build, but in no regard of similar disposition. That is to say he was a bully, and an ugly one at that, and an intellectual coward, and a common, soulless egoist, and a cur, and the last person on the planet I'd want as a companion. Still, he was always *there*, wherever I went, as if anticipating my evasions, and teasing me while claiming we were friends, and engaging me in his confidence while, at the same time, subtly threatening me. I'm sure every teen has suffered at least one episode mirroring mine. This boy confounded me to tears! For instance, were I to develop a crush on a girl, it was *he* who would badger her affections, and not relent in his advances until the girl had shied and my frustration was complete. Were I to pursue a quiet weekend, it was *he* who would show, as out of thin air, to spoil my peace. I positively loathed this boy, and found myself entertaining fantasies of trouncing him. In my dreams, too, would he appear, yet always presenting a much different temper; that of a silent, persistent, and thoroughly gloomy companion. I could not shake him in these dreams; whither I turned he was there, saying nothing, his face downcast. And always this somnolent game of turning to and fro would terminate with my facing him, unable to move. And as I would be standing, spellbound, he would be slowly shaking his head; with apology, with finality—I could never know. For as he would begin to raise his face to mine I would invariably wake screaming, and spend the rest of the night disturbing the slumber of whichever parent would have me. I began sleeping in a room where many lights were kept brightly burning, and even then slept but fitfully. At long last, my nerves in shreds, I resolved to confront this boy in a physical contest, although his natural aggressiveness made the outcome of such a confrontation a foregone conclusion. No matter. I was determined to be rid of him, despite the obviously bloody consequences. I well remember the hours spent on that smelly spit of beach beside that sodden, sagging pier, challenging myself, while unconsciously developing a muttered mantra of *"Go for the throat, go for the throat!"* Catching myself at this I desisted, and then took a strange kind of heart. Right now, from the vantage of many years, it is as if I can see my younger self through another's eyes, and observe that queer twist of the lips that is the killer's smile, on a momentarily finer boy that once was me. And so even now my withered lips convulse, and my rheumy eyes gleam, and a wan, rasping voice that is mine and is not mine whispers, "Do it! *Do it!* Go for the throat!"

I determined that this altercation would take place at the earliest opportunity, as I wanted to confront him while my courage soared. It seemed that no sooner had I made this determination than my enemy appeared walking from beneath that dank old pier, his hands thrust in his pockets, a mischievous gleam in his eye. With my blood up, I immediately lashed into him, demanding he respect my privacy, accusing him of breaches both real and imagined. To my surprise he did not become heated, but merely looked all the more mischievous. Upon that look I saw only red, and did what I had so thoroughly prepared myself to do: I went for his throat.

It was in no sense of the word a fight. Whether I overpowered him or he simply gave me free reign I can't say, for all I remember is opening my eyes to see his livid and breathless face next to mine, the gleam in those eyes nearly extinguished due to the ferocity of my chokehold. When I realized what I was doing I immediately released him and backed off. I had nearly killed the boy.

In a minute he staggered to his feet and stood looking at me oddly, struggling for breath. Finally he managed to cough out a few words, to the effect that he would get me; that I would never elude him. Thereupon he turned and rushed back under the pier. I swayed there trembling, and was quickly overcome by shame. I saw myself then as an animal, as a vile creature who pounced without provocation. I had all but murdered someone, someone whose only fault was wanting to be my friend. Brimming over with guilt and compassion, I ran across the sand into the darkness under the pier.

I expected to find him, frightened and spent, but the space under the pier appeared to be uninhabited. Calling out his name with a tone of profoundest apology, I proceeded to search the area, only to discover that I was indeed alone. I then walked to the other side of the pier, studying the sand for footprints that would establish an exit into the sunshine. Finding none, I followed up on this idea and retraced my steps to the very spot where he and I had run under the pier. *There* were his prints and mine in the glare without the shade, and *here* were mine coming into the dark and doubling back—but of his further progress there wasn't a trace. I will confess to a space of wool gathering, and then I found myself turning back to search once more. This was a silly enterprise, but the impulse was irresistible. Again finding myself alone, I stood listening to the beating of my heart, while the tide lisped softly behind me.

Then—how shall I frame it—a species of qualm that was not altogether new shook me like a dog. I mean to say that I trembled head to toe in one long excruciating wave, as if a block of ice had just rolled down my spine. I could not turn, I could not move, I could not think. And I stood there in the dark letting my eyes adjust, and *feeling* the presence of another. It was not a sensation of touch, but of the coldest scrutiny. I don't think I took a breath for the better part of a minute, while this presence slowly moved around me, as though taking me in from all sides. At last I broke, and ran back out into the summer glare. I remember standing there blinking, trying to put two and two together. I had an odd impression that something was stirring under the pier, but, whatever it was, it was as insubstantial as the wind. This impression of activity seemed to work its way to the very edge of shadow, and again I had that chilling sense of being observed. I stood transfixed, staring at nothing. Then I supposed I perceived, again, a mantle; a ghostly outline, but more detailed, and further extended than that similar apparition which had so thrilled me as a child. I was aware of a fleeting *intensity*. And all at once I felt I was being strangled. I might have been dangling from a gallows. In a minute the feeling passed, and left me peering into a space of unoccupied shadow.

This experience shook me for years, and while I never saw that particular boy again, I was very reserved in subsequent relationships. Time always heals. It dilutes feelings, rearranges memories. But at the subconscious level something vital *remembers*. Odd patterns, strangely familiar, strike deep chords. The self-preservation instinct never rests. And it keeps me watchful. Trust is for the godly and the guileless.

In this way have I kept my mind intact over all these years. I have learned to sleep in the daytime, and only then in wide open spaces, lest even one long finger of shadow sneak upon me. Nights are spent indoors, with all lights burning.

Of course I was considered eccentric. And, later on, even mad. Those sent to interview me always showed their hand; none dared meet my challenge, none dared speak with me away from edifice or mound—away from things that will *cast*. And so have I endured.

The state's awkward advances have actually worked in my favor. They have decided my mind is unbalanced, and so awarded me monthly checks and medication. Their neatly pre-scribed poisons I flush immediately. Their saccharine represent-atives I have worn down; I will be interviewed only in this open expanse of public park, and only on this very bench.

I had a wife. For the space of a year. And during that restless year the woman grew sicker almost daily. I watched the light *seep* from her face. I was not an altogether obsessed man in those days, and still had essential needs and pursuits. But even *she*, in due course, became suspect. She had supposed me insane. Perhaps she was right in stating that I took whatever she said out of context. But I knew she was tainted. At length I could not bear her to sit in the dark. The woman was tainted. Thank God we had no children.

When she was buried I stipulated that her gravesite should not be in the proximity of willow or statue—of anything that might throw a shadow. I am not mad. I need not state this emphatically, for I have a lifetime of empirical proof to stead me. I am not mad—I am punctilious. I plainly see that which any man, should he look hard enough, will easily be made to ascertain. And so I can very *reasonably* state that that woman was placed, and that she most certainly *was* tainted.

Do not misapprehend me here.

There are precisely two aspects, no more, to this intoxicating thunderclap we call reality.

One is that acknowledged world of surface and substance; absolutely familiar, brightly lit and amenable to perception.

The other is a cold and thirsty place, discernible only to the blind. It is no less real than the sensory world we accept, and is as deep as the cosmos. It is the unseen. It leaches us all; continuously, insidiously, surely. It is vital entropy, lurking in every lost moment, in every broken heart, behind every fixed idea; waiting to reveal itself at that single horrible, drawn-out moment when we are no longer dazzled by the light.

We are too involved to realize we are, fundamentally, masters of nothing. Only our arrogance allows us to accept this instantaneous *affront* of light, of life, as a matter of worth. Only ego makes nonchalance possible. We are being snuffed, you and I. But so gradually as to be unaware.

And now, as I sit on this bench in the giving sun, what bothers me most is that I alone should be privy to this duality, this presence, this...this outrage. Other men are inspired by a variety of muses. Other men, in appearance no different than I, labor after strange appliances, build empires, surrender their selves to families and friends. Only I, it would seem, have been cursed with this dark insight.

But I am not mad. I only wish I were. At any rate, this argument is academic. I have looked long enough, and looked hard enough, to determine the full lineament of that which resides in shade. It peers from the depths of a million misgivings, and whispers in that soft pad of approaching steps.

I am old—so old. Why have I had to wait *so* long for the inevitable...why be born at all? To merely pass from the prenatal state of nonexistence into this brief and draining glare; to exist for a blinding heartbeat, only to pass back into shadow...I will not look. I do not have to. For, I tell you, I am not mad! And I *hear* those footsteps. And I *see* that coming shadow. And I *know* the face behind that cold hand on my shoulder. It is you; it is you who watch from the doorwells, you who venture in the night. You, you, and you; the selfish, the venal, the hard of heart. May you burn in the light I am leaving. May you find shade enough in the grave.

Justman

"Hermie, me hearty, by the time I get a few rufies in that little bimbo she's gonna know the Ol' Shaman is pure Prescription X."

The table was bumped—*precisely* as a pair of samples were being physically juxtaposed in an A/B comparison. The specimens, thus roughly mixed on the handler's palms, produced a stinging sensation and an unfamiliar, nauseating odor.

When Richard Dukhedd smelled that odor he looked up from his table with a most uncharacteristic snarl. His nostrils flared repeatedly, his eyes burned in haunted caves. A string of saliva rolled off his lip.

The expression was so savage both lab assistants stopped dead in their tracks. After a minute the bigmouth wondered, "Hey, Dickhead! What's with you? You look like you just wolfed down a Mama Cass." To his accomplice he said, in a jocular aside, "That's our catering truck's ham and chile relleno with heavy tabasco."

Dukhedd pulled himself together, surprised by the recent feeling's intensity, and ventured meekly, "Er, it's *Dukhedd*." He remembered he had to remind this particular lab boy every single blessed working day of his life. For some reason that stuck in his craw. Strange. He'd never realized he had a craw.

"Okay, *Dickhead*." The assistant nudged the other boy, a new face at Chemright. "Herman Wilson, this is good old Ducky Dickhead. Here he sits, slaving away every day without complaining. That nameplate there is actually his headstone. See? 'Ducky Dickhead. Born God knows when. Lived God knows why. Died facedown in a puddle of cheap perfume for some woman who wouldn't give him the time of day.' Is that what you're working on today, Dickhead? Another of those groovy little scents the boss's squeeze is so crazy about? When are you gonna hit him up for a raise, man? Tell his wife about the squeeze. Or, better yet, just walk right in and tell him you know all about it. Then watch the red carpet treatment!"

"Why, yes," Dukhedd said absently. "I was just cross-analyzing pheromone samples of a motorcycle outlaw and a ground ape. Unfortunately they seem to have become intermingled here. But not to worry. Doctor Weissman has plenty of simian semen in storage, and I can always go back to that tavern restroom for more outlaw specimens." The thought revolted him. It had been terribly difficult getting through that crowd last night, and several of the brutes had accosted him when they caught him scraping the stall walls for samples. Dukhedd rubbed the lump on the back of his head and remembered the gauntlet of pool cues and hairy bellies. Every window on his dusty orange Pacer had been smashed, and the stench of rolling troglodytes had clung to him all the way home. The dry cleaners had refused to accept his clothes.

"Well, good for you, yo-yo. You just keep mixing away there, Dickhead, and maybe someday they'll name something particularly smelly after you. Come on, Hermie, old boy, let me introduce you to the Broom Closet. It's where you go to sneak a smoke or smoke a secretary."

The two laughed and kicked their way through the swinging doors leading to Warehouse. Dukhedd watched them go with narrowed eyes. His palms burned and itched, his shoulders kept fighting to remake his posture into a headlong crouch. He rose slowly, crept to the settling double doors, and peered through the right-hand pane. The lab boys were halfway across Warehouse, heading for a little door Dukhedd knew led to a sleepy room stocked with miscellaneous supplies and equipment. Barely aware of his actions, he slipped inside and stepped up to an in-building intercom, flicked a switch and said, *"Herman Wilson to Inventory, please. Herman Wilson to Inventory."* Dukhedd watched as the Wilson boy looked around fearfully. He saw the bigmouth josh him confidently, and then Wilson was hurrying for the doors at West End. The bigmouth, Dukhedd suddenly remembered, was named Perigas. Evan Perigas. He stared angrily as Perigas pulled out a pack of smokes and made his way to the Broom Closet. Now Dukhedd, almost as a conditioned response, slipped between the tall racks and began following him one row at a time.

Warehouse was deserted. Once Perigas had snuck into the room and closed the door, Dukhedd was able to boldly step forward. Right then, Chemright's least appreciated wunderkind couldn't have explained himself if you put a gun to his head. He only knew his destiny waited in that room, just behind that little wood door he was fast approaching with his body in a crouch and his palms itching like crazy.

At the last moment Dukhedd stopped on a dime, turned the knob quietly, and eased open the door. As Warehouse light fell on him, Perigas immediately dropped his lit cigarette and covered it with a shoe. When he realized it was only Dukhedd his startled expression became one of contempt and resentment.

"Dickhead! You damned meddler! What are you doing snooping around here, anyway?"

"You," Dukhedd responded, his voice growing in intensity with every syllable, "are a very bad man, and unfit to be a member of the gene pool." This little utterance amazed him. He'd never spoken a harsh word in his life. A shudder ran up and down his body. The Broom Closet filled with a muskiness somehow both infuriating and intoxicating.

"And *you*," Perigas scowled, "are unfit to lick my boots. So checkmate." He lit a fresh cigarette, but in the glare of the match saw something in Dukhedd's face that made him step back. Dukhedd's expression seemed to be trying to find its place, scrunching and writhing all about before finally settling into one of rabid psychosis. "Now hold on there, Dukhedd," Perigas mumbled. "Richard."

"Unfit," Dukhedd slobbered. "Gene pool."

"Hold it!" Perigas shot, and grabbed a heavy-duty box cutter from a table. He thumbed open the blade. Before he knew it, Dukhedd had swiped it from his hand and was advancing menacingly.

"Un...*fit!*" Dukhedd snarled, clamping a wildly itching palm over Perigas's mouth. He slammed the assistant's head on the floor and held it while cutting open the boy's trousers. A brief flurry of denim and blood spattered the Broom Closet's near wall. "Unfit," Dukhedd swore, unaware of the shrieking gusts bursting from Perigas's nostrils, "unfit...*gene pool!*"

The castration was very swift, very unscientific, and very messy. Perigas passed out screaming, leaving Dukhedd slumped with the blade in one hand and the lab assistant's manhood in the other. There was blood everywhere. As rational thought returned, Dukhedd gradually became aware of his plight. He was also aware he'd taken the first step on a momentous journey. There was important work to be done—under no circumstances must Perigas be allowed to blow his cover. Grabbing the unconscious assistant by the hair, Dukhedd coldly snapped back his head, located the jugular, and brought the blade down.

"Hold it right there," said the burly man at the door. "Don't I know you? I think I know you." He held a gnarly hand in front of Dukhedd's face. Tattooed across the back of the hand was the legend, ME ASHOL. Dukhedd's eyes followed a series of tattooed arrows leading up a fat hairy arm, across a fat hairy shoulder, and so on up to a fat hairy forehead bearing the second half of the message: YOO DED! Ordinarily the nauseating odor produced by this massive individual would have made Dukhedd dizzy and weak, but now it only engendered a snarl and tensing of the shoulders. His palms began to itch. His fingers clenched.

The brute's head cocked backward at that snarl, and his hand shot up to study the back of Dukhedd's skull. "Why, it's you, all right. I remember you from last night. You're the funny little fellow we played foosball with, all the way out into the parking lot."

"Dukhedd," the funny little fellow said out of habit. "Richard Percival Dukhedd. I'll, er, be getting out of your way now." Something abruptly straightened his back, and his voice, in that quirkily masculine tone he'd fallen into of late, said, "But not this time, I won't." Before Dukhedd could make a move, he was compelled to explain himself (after that nasty little incident with Perigas he'd come to his senses quickly, his self-preservation instinct burning red-hot. He'd cleaned himself up very carefully in the employee's lounge lavatory before returning to his desk, pontificating under his breath all the way. No one suspected gentle Dukhedd of course; he hadn't even been detained for questioning. Herman Wilson, the last person seen with a living Perigas, was presently under house arrest and close observation. Chemright had been shut down for the investigation into the lab boy's brutal murder, and everybody sent home). Without having to collect his thoughts, Dukhedd now said, "Mister Biker, because you are a deliberate insult to every standard of decency devised by intelligent men, you are about to experience the exquisite horror of waking in the emergency room. So please pay attention:

"Sin number one: you believe obnoxiousness is cool. For this snub at five thousand years of the civilizing process you will spend the rest of your life attached to a colostomy bag.

"Sin number two: you think masculinity is a quality best defined by foul and offensive behavior, and that grease, din, and deviancy are elements to admire.

"Sin number three: you feel that intimidating those less massive makes you a superior specimen. And for this little travesty you will learn to operate a wheelchair from the ground up, so to speak. So say '*Vroom vroom*,' Mister 'Big Bad Biker,' and get ready to meet your new set of wheels."

The hairy man's jaw dropped, his beady eyes narrowed. But before he could signal his lurking horde, Dukhedd had spun him around, ripped down his pants, and yanked out a good eighteen inches of descending colon. He stepped over the writhing ashol and elbowed his way inside the bar.

Dozens of similar hulking creeps were gathered in drunken packs; Dukhedd recognized many of them from last night. When the meanest loped up with pool cue in hand, Dukhedd calmly ripped off his face and threw the oozing flesh mask like a Frisbee into the crowd. He kicked the screaming man in the scrotum twice for every scream until the racket ceased.

"Now," Dukhedd said, pulling a pair of ice tongs from under his lab coat, "one of you lucky ashols is just about to graciously volunteer a semen sample. I'll make the collection process short and sweet. Then I'll be getting out of your way."

The Ford Ranger came up on his bumper again, so close the ashol's face was right in Dukhedd's rear-view mirror. Dukhedd grimaced as the night's hard-won sample rolled precariously on the dash. The Ranger tried to pass at a bottleneck, almost taking out the Pacer's right-rear panel. Dukhedd sped up and veered to the right, forcing the ashol to back off. He couldn't help it; his rage at this dangerous display of selfishness in a social situation, at night with no law enforcement around, grew with each yank of the wheel. The Ranger began honking insistently—how dare a little orange Pacer with no glass be in the superior ashol's way.

Dukhedd's shoulders were hunched, his knuckles white on the steering wheel. As the Ranger pulled right up on the Pacer's rear bumper, Dukhedd gradually slowed.

The ashol was barely able to avoid an unflattering ding on his own, finer bumper. He held his palm down on the horn, but Dukhedd only slowed further, until the inferior little Pacer was controlling the pace of the two vehicles at around fifteen miles per hour.

That continuous blare of horn was drilling through Dukhedd's skull, but his focus did not falter. His eyes shot left and right. There were no cars around; only the few red jewels of taillights a quarter mile ahead, petering quickly as the Pacer and Ranger slowed.

Dukhedd forced a complete stop. Each adamant blast of the Ranger's horn caused his neck to sink an inch deeper between his bunching shoulders. When he heard the Ranger's door slam his palms were itching so badly the Pacer's steering wheel was like ground glass. Every approaching footstep was another twist of the gonads, each challenging expletive sweet music to the ear. When the ashol reached the Pacer's door, Dukhedd came out of the driver's window like toothpaste out of a tube. He put one fist straight into the ashol's adam's apple, felt the jelly knob sunder into mush. "For brashness are you silenced," he hissed. He crushed the ashol's spine like a beer can. "For arrogance are you diminished." He kicked and kicked and kicked the ashol's cadaver until it was impressed into the Ranger's grille. "Solely for display purposes are you here."

Dukhedd blanched at the news. He was all over AM radio, his name mispronounced and his character misrepresented. Another anchor reported that a Richard Percival Dickhead was wanted for questioning in the Chemright incident—and that one Herman Wilson, recently released from custody, had informed detectives of Dickhead's confessed strategy just minutes before the assault in question. Dukhedd pounded his fist on the Pacer's peeling plastic steering wheel cover, visualizing he and Wilson in all manner of bloody scenarios.

A ruckus to his right snapped him out of it. In Cartwheel's new Cellular Mall, dozens of loping gangbangers were chasing down a little man in a bright orange costume. Dukhedd hit the brakes even as another group cut the man off. The whole mess swarmed him; fists, feet, furheads—everywhere! Never in his life had Dukhedd deliberately enjoined an altercation, but the sight of this helpless fleeing victim, in the very process of being mauled by a fresh leash of ashols, threw his blood pressure into orbit. He was hyperventilating; tiny feral gasps whistled out his nostrils. The seatbelt refused to comply; Dukhedd ripped it from its moorings. The driver's door was jammed (one biker had head-butted the Pacer); Dukhedd kicked it free. He grabbed the keys, arranged them to protrude separately between the fingers of his closed fist, and sprinted into the mob, jabbing eyes into jelly, julietting lips, making bloomin' onions of noses. A number of dullards made to retaliate and—Dukhedd lost it completely. By the time he reached the supine little man it was a gangbanger's graveyard, and sirens were carving holes in the distance.

Dukhedd rolled him onto his back. He was a dweeby stiff, not unlike his rescuer. Dukhedd scooped him up and raced to the Pacer before the cops could make a mess out of a miracle. He laid him on the front seat, fanned the face and rubbed the limbs. In a minute the eyelids fluttered. A scrawny hand shot upward, grabbed Dukhedd by the lapel. "Gene pool," the dweeb mumbled. Dukhedd nodded passionately. The hand dropped. "I," the little man managed, "have eradicated my share of stoopuds."

Dukhedd nodded harder. "Ashols," he translated.

"It is time to pass the torch." The man's voice was wind through leaves. Again with the hand to the lapel, again with the trailing mantra. "I sought a successor; instead has he succumbed to me." Dukhedd had to move his ear right down to the man's pale rolling lips. "Long have I labored," the dweeb went on, "seeking a cure for the source of moral retardation that has plagued our race since its inception. I was this close." He held up a shakily parted forefinger and thumb. His head rolled to the side. He looked dead. "Magnets!" he spewed, and gripped Dukhedd's wrist with passion. "Oh, for the love of God—the derelicts, the gayboys, the harlots, the televangelists…" He was clearly delirious.

"Gene pool!" Dukhedd sobbed, his head rolling miserably. "Yes. Yes."

"I was shittin'," the little man gasped. He shook his head in frustration. "Smitten, kitten, mitten—I was bitten, bitten by a honey badger that had previously stepped in a certain muscle-headed governor's urine. Oh, the humanity…it is pheromones! Pheromones control our every slip and brute desire. Well, perhaps not you and I, but all these barbaric marauders, all the venal charlatans who dictate our lives, all the wezls and horz yanking and cranking and shanking and watching our every weakness. Oh, the magnets!"

Dukhedd wept as he nodded. "Gene pool."

"You must take this uniform. You must wear it with pride as you combat the wezls and horz, the doprz and loitrz; the stoopuds in general."

"Ashols," Dukhedd said. He peered at the man's costume doubtfully, less than enthused by the prospect of battling evil while looking like a Dreamsicle.

"This is to be your guide." The dweeb pulled a battered thesaurus from a marsupial breast pocket, handed it to Dukhedd. "I," he gurgled, "am Justman!" A shudder ran up and down his frame. "*You…are Justman!*"

Dukhedd buried him that night, on a knoll beneath the mall's giant phone logo. He tried the costume on and found it five sizes too small, itchy in the crotch and pits, and prone to clinging in the least appropriate places. But it was an outstanding color match for the Pacer, and this coincidence alone made him ponder the serpentine role of Destiny. The dweeb's words glowed on his mind's back burner: *"Instead has he succumbed to me."* Dukhedd navigated the mean streets of Cartwheel with a whole new attitude.

That night Dukhedd hunched in a 7-11 parking lot, poring over the thesaurus under a dome light's dimming sallow haze. The Pacer was out of gas, Dukhedd out of cash, and it really didn't matter—he was thunderstruck; not only by the extensive marginalia, but by the book itself.

Roget did something stunningly straightforward way back in 1852; he categorized nouns in direct relation to their antonyms. Dukhedd's ex-bookshelf consisted mainly of chemistry tomes and spiral-bound olfactory charts, and the only thesaurus he'd thumbed was one of the popular editions featuring the "arranged just like a dictionary!" bullshit. Roget's original wasn't concerned with the abc cretins; it was designed to elucidate.

Good man, Dukhedd read, and rolled his eyes to the opposing column. *Bad man*. Dukhedd blinked. Absolutely sound. *Virtue*. And its antonym, *Vice. Kindness. Cruelty. Honor, Dishonor. Loyalty, Treachery. Justice*—and here Dukhedd had to stop, squinting in the sudden seizure of overlapping addenda. Scrawled in black ink were the words: ~~Rightman, Goodman, Virtueman,~~ and the bold and italicized, ***Justman!*** Dukhedd now noticed circled words, and a faint and wobbly, imposed skeletal sub-frame. Beneath *Bad Man* was the scribble WEZL, beneath *Bad Woman* the legend HOR. Dukhedd nodded. The banner for the sub-frame was the coined STOOPUD. He understood. Dukhedd fingered the orange costume with a new respect.

"Yo yo yo, homey. Yo be up wit some change in da hood?"

The voice in his ear was like sandpaper. Dukhedd had to rub his palms hard on the Pacer's abraded seat cover. His head ratcheted to the left.

"What it be cracka? Yo be in da flicky wit da bling bling?"

"Wezl," Dukhedd breathed.

"*What?* See-it! I jus be jammin in da foo schoo, yo digs? Jus a dollah, dog." A squeege clattered around the Pacer's windowless frame.

That was enough. Dukhedd's left arm shot out and brought back a handful of Bad Man. He stuffed the screaming wezl in the glovebox, appendage by appendage, until there was only the squashed remains of its trousers in his hand. Odd: He palpated a hefty lump in a space that should have contained only air. Dukhedd peeled back the fabric to reveal a wad of bills crammed in a leather tobacco pouch. Gas money, food money, and more. Enough to launch the new Justman. Dukhedd rolled the Pacer out the drive and into the street. There was an all-night gas station only two miles up the Grapevine. He took the steering wheel in one hand, the crushed door in the other, and began to shove.

Everybody now knows the final leg of the Justman saga. Friends still argue the good and the bad, the right and the wrong, the dos and the don'ts. Bullies are prone to think twice before picking on geeks, perverts tend to keep it all indoors. The gleeful bludgeoning of religious hypocrites, we all agree, must cease at once.

Yet there are times when we can't help but fondly recall the mechanics forced to perform surgeries on doctors, the lawyers forced to dismantle and rebuild the vehicles of mechanics, the systematic and long overdue barbecuing of Death Row inmates. Who can forget the thousands of shamelessly dressed horz, hung naked from street lamps over Dobermans in heat, or the endless packs of street wezls, violently indroctrinated into a lifetime of community service? The politicians dressed in leotards and rainbow wigs, the horrified low riders, strapped in bumper cars set to prestissimo...the bitch-slapped gang-bangers...all the rude cell phone yammerers with their tongues expunged...the professional athletes in silk underwear, rolling beach balls with their noses on a spectator-packed, glass-enclosed, and fittingly shallow field of dreams.

Was Justman a villain, as the hookers, realtors, and telemarketers like to proclaim? Or was he really a hero, doing what we sorry-don't-want-to-get-involved rubbernecks only wish we had the gonads to enjoin?

From that first mass return-punting of border jumpers to his final group batoning by itchy Police Cadets, the story shall remain a mystery, for Justman himself granted no interviews, and was tightlipped about the whole phenomenon, other than the trademark pithy explanations preceding each protracted measure of Justice. He is known to have produced a single in-depth explanation on the ultimate consequence of Evil, and for this mighty exposition we have one Herman Wilson, still in shock from the sulfuric acid, the cattleprods, and that televised and oft-parodied naked citywide meat hook ride.

But Hermie ain't talking.

The Gloaming

*If I live to see another tomorrow, I swear—never again!
I don't care how many times I've made that promise, or how
many times I've broken it, this hangover* will *be the last. Unto
that vow I hereby dedicate this unbelievable headache and
what's left of these sinuses. I waive my right to the pursuit of
happiness, and bequeath my folly to the next poor sap with a
strange chick's waist in one hand and the debris of his pay-
check in the other. I'm done, man. I surrender. Hand me an AM
radio and a good book. From now on it's green tea and whole
wheat toast.*

*Let's see. There's a foot; still got one, two, three, four—
all five toes. Then that must be my other foot in that crusty shoe
with the bloody sock. Simple enough: swing the leg with the
bare foot off the couch, like...so, then follow it with the other
leg. Now we just sit up and—*

*No! Don't try that again. Regulate your breathing. What
was that you once read about drunks drowning in their own
vomit? Relax...roll onto your side...draw up your knees. Now
very* carefully *pull your upper body into a sitting position.*

There you go. Rather like being on a tilt-a-whirl, but that'll clear up when you open your eyes...one, two, three, four—go!

Christ, what a mess. I live here*? I've been robbed! Who tore down the curtains? My TV! Who kicked in the screen? I'll kill him, I'll murder the whole lot of 'em! There's the other shoe. Slide in a throbbing foot; can't commit mayhem gimping all over town with only one shoe. But oh please; just let me lay down a bit first. Let me get my strength back. Not that—not the puke again!* Can't *lay down. I'll die, man, I'll die. Take something quick. Pepto Bismol. Baking soda. Something for the gut. In the bathroom. In...the bathroom! Fast!*

I'm sure I can remember making it to the bathroom doorway. I still see myself weaving there, balancing the odds of finding the sink and losing it right where I stood. And I vividly recall a crazy smash as the living room window blew in. I turned in amazement, and in that one brief glimpse I've never been soberer.

The thing that lurched over the TV was wild, man, was worse than any nightmare. I saw a skeletal frame, hollow eyes, fiery hair...it was hysterical—it was screaming like a bobcat.

I did what anybody would do. I slammed and locked the door. I slid trembling to the floor. I began to blubber like a child facing his first dentist. A second later fists were frantically hammering up and down the door. It occurred to me even then, freaked out as I was, that the knob wasn't tried. I leapt on the bureau beside the basin, kicked out both foot-square panes, and shot out the window headfirst.

I took a mouthful out of the carport's gravel roof. But before I hit I saw a world gone mad; creatures identical to that thing now breaking in the bathroom door, houses and a-partments on fire, savaged bodies scattered amidst cars and dragged-out furniture.

A man doesn't do a whole lot of analyzing under these circumstances, and anyway, in my case nature wasn't all that generous with the gray matter. I was no great shakes as an athlete either; I twisted an ankle and almost broke my neck shimmying down a drain pipe. Was it only yesterday I was bragging about what a hot jock of a salesman I was? Fat lot of good that did me now.

Ducking into the carport brought on a wave of ambivalence; I felt both shade-secreted and hopelessly socked in. A number of those things were visible in the street—and now two more were loping across the drive—but they couldn't stop half a ton of screaming metal. I crept on hands and knees to my Accord's door, silently turned the key in the lock, and slipped inside.

The creature that got right in my face nearly stopped my heart. As the wave of hair lashed my eyes I threw up my arms against a hail of fists and snapping teeth. I felt those teeth tear into my hand, and had just time to see it was a young Latina—a real human, like me, but one making an awful lot of noise—before my good hand balled into a fist and doubled her over the seat into the back. She was out before she hit the upholstery.

At the sound of the engine turning over, the things in the drive whirled and made right for me. Thank God Accords don't need to warm—I punched it out of the carport and scattered the first two like 7-and 9 pins.

On the road I was the going attraction—every vehicle was dead, crashed, or a smoking ruin. Those things came running out of buildings and leaping from fire escapes, screaming strangely and throwing their arms. It was still too hectic to get a good long look at one, but they were all skeletal and blood-red, with plentiful scalp fur, and with tufts on the forearms, backs, and ankles.

Downtown was a fresh vision of Hell. Mangled and mutilated people all over the place, a dog torn to ribbons still protecting its master's corpse, an overturned school bus full of screaming children trying to fight off a dozen monsters hammering on the undercarriage like gulls on a barnacle. Fires everywhere; in stores, in theaters and churches. In less than ten minutes I was on the backroads.

A groan behind me took my mind out of the whirl. I pulled over.

The woman was nursing her swollen jaw. I must have knocked out a molar; there was blood tamping the inside of her lips. I yanked her up by the hair.

"Do you speak English?"

She moaned something unintelligible.

"Do you speak English?" I showed her my fist again.

"Yes, yes! Si! Don't hit me!"

"What's going on around here? What are those things?"

"I don't know. I woke up and they were everywhere. Don't hit me!"

I unballed my fist and tried to relax. "What do you mean you 'woke up.' How could anybody sleep through all that?"

Her expression fell. "I...I wasn't asleep. I took some pills. To help me."

"To help you sleep?"

She pushed my arm away. "To help me stop living. ¿Comprende? Is that kosher-clear enough for you?"

I turned back, bristling. "Next time try carbon monoxide." Every other radio station featured a self-repeating alert, full of pings and droning mayorese. A few were so disorganized it was impossible to tell what was taking place at the stations. One gave a monotonous human patter.

"What's he saying?"

"I don't speak freaking Farsi."

I glared into the rear-view mirror. "But you freaking recognized it as freaking Farsi, didn't you?"

"This time," the woman hissed, "black my eyes! That way I won't have to freaking look at you." She turned her head. "Puerco."

I blew out a sigh. "Look, I'm genuinely sorry I socked you. You were making enough noise to get us killed. And you bit the hell out of my hand."

"You sneaked up on me."

"You were in my car."

"Yeah? Well, this is where I get out of your car."

I reached back. She swatted my arm as I yanked the handle and threw open the door. "Then freaking *get* out."

She looked around doubtfully, and for a quirky moment was just a girl without a daddy. When she turned back the fire had retaken her eyes.

"You'd really kick me out? You'd leave me to die? What are you, an animal?"

I slammed the door. "Two things. One, you said you wanted out. Two, you were all set to die anyway. I'm glad you've had a change of heart. Let's see if we can work this thing through together." There was an uncomfortable pause. "What's your name?"

The eyes burned up at me. "Chiquita. What's yours?"

I turned back to face the road, my hands clutching the wheel. "Hymie," I muttered, and rammed the car into drive.

The city's outskirts contained far fewer of those gaunt furry things. We saw the occasional stalker prowling the fields like a plains hunter, going after field mice perhaps. They only showed in pairs where a kill was in progress, and stared dumbly at the passing Accord. My hangover was back. I was trying to piece together the paucity of available data; nothing was conclusive. I noted a burnt umber cast to the noon sky, a high-pitched drone that went on and on just at the threshold of awareness, a vaguely rotten-egg stench all around. My lips tingled. Finally I got a broadcast that was certainly in Spanish.

"There! What's that lady saying?"

No answer.

I looked back as I drove. "Come on! We're in this to-gether."

She glowered in her slump. "She say Jewboy pack uno mean punch."

"Damn you!" I stared straight ahead.

After a minute she appended, "And she says Jesus Christo has come to lead us home. That was a rosary you just heard. No news. Just prayers. Who do you pray to?"

"You know damn well who I pray to." We were coming into a little town. It appeared deserted. "Look, I don't know about you, but I've got one hell of a headache. I'm going for the hair of the dog; there's a market right up there. Besides, we'll need food, gas, and some kind of weapon. I'll dash in while you wait in the car with the motor running." Immediately I was struck by the folly of this little notion. "Look who I'm talking to." I pictured myself coming out to find the car long gone. "I'm taking the keys with me." I blinked rapidly, now visualizing her laughing inside with the doors locked, holding down the latch while I furiously tried the key. My brain was a tender bruise. "You're coming with me."

"I don't get a vote?"

"No, you don't get a vote. You're coming along or this ride is history."

We opened our doors simultaneously. "Don't lock it," I whispered. "We may need that extra second."

The odor and whine were much more pronounced once we'd stepped out. Also, the air burned our eyes. The market was vacated, the shelves and freezer intact. We were loading up on essentials when I found the shopkeeper's remains behind the counter. It was so bad I threw up there and then. The woman poured water on my head while running ice cubes along the back of my neck.

"Don't look at it any more. Drink some of this. Little sips! Don't take big swallows."

I got down some water, rinsed and spat.

She leaned over the counter, said, "He put up a fight," and came back with a bloody crowbar. "Maybe we can use this." While I slumped getting my wind she went through the hardware section in the back. When she returned she was carrying a couple of propane torches and extra canisters. "Weapons." She picked up a butane lighter.

A scratch and clacking outside.

In two seconds I had the door closed. Half a minute later I'd barricaded it with everything from a steel shelf to a keg of nails.

"Loo…" called a voice. In the distance rose a high-pitched reply. "Loo?"

There was a similar clacking within the store, just inside the little back room. I swear my heart stopped at that moment; it's not just a saying. Somewhere between the last beat and the next, the ajar back door flew inward and one of those things shot in screaming.

If not for that woman I'd be hamburger right now. Without batting an eye, she lit the torch, cranked up the gas, and stuck it right in that death's head face. The fur went up like balled confetti as it staggered out the way it came.

I grabbed the stuffed bags and kicked away my amateurish little barricade. It might seem strange we were so quick to head into that freak show, but there's a weird underlying component to human nature—no matter how worse the subsequent situation, we simply had to get *out* of that store.

They were all over the place; stepping from behind bushes, roosting on my car. The woman went at them with a lit torch in each hand, stabbing the flames in their faces, mirroring their screams. In this way we made it to the Accord. She really went at them at the door; I had to plead to get her inside.

"They don't like fire!" I exulted as she slammed her door.

"Nobody does."

I threw it in drive and swerved on out of there, recklessly, and probably needlessly; they were wary of moving vehicles.

We hurtled through the little town. At length I relaxed. "I see you're still on your suicide trip. But you've got balls for a skirt; I'll give you that much." I tried to come off conversationally. "You never did tell me why you took those pills."

She grabbed my arm. "Stop! Sign!"

I shook off her hand. "I know what a stop sign looks like! *Never* touch a man's driving arm."

She punched that driving arm so hard I'll have a bruise if I live to see Chanukha. She knew just where to connect, too; it was that tender spot on the right bicep invariably selected by bullies. She probably learned it from scrapping with her chicken farm hermanos. I despise tomboys.

"Not a stop sign, you retard. Look!"

Tied to a leaning gnarly oak was a home-made banner, proclaiming,

IF U CAN RED THIS COM TO FORTH STRET AND ABEL
STRET. WE AR HERE FOR U. FOOD AND SHELTR. JESUS
IS THE WA.

"Turn here!" she commanded.

"I *know* where I'm going!"

The closer we came to Fourth and Abel, the heavier grew the presence of those predatory creatures. At the address—a Chevron station—there was a mob of 'em. In a blaze of retaliatory machismo, I shot straight through a broad gap and screeched to a halt at the office door, ready to peel right back out as soon as that uncharacteristic little blaze had been properly snuffed. All the windows were smashed, but the repair bay's steel sliding door promptly rolled up on protesting pulleys. Out sprang an elderly man and woman. They grabbed us and hustled us inside. The steel door slammed to the cement.

The interior was illuminated by a hundred candles; some free-standing, some scented votives. The brick walls were now finger-painted murals of crucifixion scenes in colored chalk, interspersed with Christian clichés scrawled in used motor oil. There were maybe two dozen nervous citizens huddled centripetally. They ran the gamut—everything from truck drivers to welfare moms.

"Bless you!" breathed the old man, eagerly echoed by frantic nods from his wisp of a wife. They clasped our hands with the wont of their genders. "We were beginning to fear we were the sole survivors. But come; you must be famished. Sit with us and freely partake of the Lord's beneficence." He motioned to a table peppered with the contents of the station crew's break room. I saw Oreos, pretzels, and two six-packs of Diet-Rite. Cheetos and Top Ramen, a few pouches of instant hot chocolate.

"We've got stuff," I mumbled, "in the car. You're welcome to it. More important is news. Like, what's going on? How did this all come about? What are those things out there?"

"These are questions," the old woman said, "which must be put to Jesus."

Out of the corner of my eye I noticed my worse half, shaking her head emphatically while resting a palm on her head to imply a yamulka.

"I saw that!" I bowed to our little white-haired host. "You'll forgive my friend's problems with basic communication. English is her second language. Now, what news have you? And why no lights?"

"The power is gone," the old man grieved. "Still, we have the light of our Lord."

"What about the emergency generators?"

The old couple traded timid looks.

"¡Ay, caramba!" came a voice at my side, and my shotgun walked into the break room to pry open a steel wall panel.

In a minute there was a muffled kick and surge. Artificial light flooded the room. She strolled back in. "Okay. The pump switches are on. This place isn't a church; it's a crypt. You people will starve to death in here. At least outside you've got a shot."

Our hosts began to argue feebly, but there was no doubt they were outvoted. The whole crowd grabbed their belongings and lined up at the big sliding door.

"You make things look easy," I muttered, with a grudging admiration I couldn't disguise. "Too easy."

"I try harder. Can you handle this mob?"

"I guess. What do you want me to do?" Did I just say that?

"Listen up," she called. "This is the man you want to hang with." She inclined her head. "No offense, mamacita and papa. We're all gonna stay bunched in a group. It's what little fish do when they want a bigger fish to back off. There's trucks and trailers in the parking lot. We're going to blast our way out of here like gangbusters and look for a safer haven. This is not a random suggestion being put to a vote. Grab your gear and get ready."

"What about weapons?" I maundered. "If those critters catch us in here with the gate up—"

"Get away from the door." She stood on her toes, grabbed the chain, and gave it one long meaningful yank. "Blow it on out of here!" As the door rolled up, everybody hunched, squinted, and inched out in a tight group.

The things were all ringed at a respectable distance; I got the impression they were sick of beating themselves silly on that impenetrable sliding door. As they watched us proceed, a common clacking and cooing filled the air.

There came a familiar light thrumming high overhead. We all looked up. It was a small plane, maybe a Cessna, winging west on an updraft. The brutes all craned their gnarly necks, and a great cheer went up on the ground. The plane appeared to dip in acknowledgement. A minute later it was a speck.

"Maybe he'll be back," someone cried.

The woman at my side turned sarcastically. "Would *you* be coming back?" She was really starting to bug me; in the way she intuitively took forward steps, whether in deed or in patter. I guess it was simple envy—me crouching there with my panties all in a bunch—but that kind of alpha behavior doesn't typically cross genders. As if to accentuate our relationship, she shove-punched me in the shoulder blade.

"That guy's got the right idea. We have to get off the ground. There's a poquito airport over there." She smacked me upside the head to make sure I was following.

"I *know* where it is!"

"You get in the Accord." She turned to address the crowd. "Everybody pile into that U-Haul. Homeboy, you're driving. When I give the signal, you U-haulass out of here. Head for the sticks and keep on heading."

"What signal?" called a little woman in the back.

"This." She yanked a nozzle off a pump, held it high in one hand and the disposable lighter in the other.

Tough to describe the compound squeal that went up as those church mice fell over one another in their scramble for the U-Haul. She watched them pile in the back like border-jumpers prodded by a coyote. I shivered at the wheel. When the truck's sliding rear panel slammed down she turned and blew a kiss at the approaching creatures.

"Come on, babies. Mama's waiting. Come here, my sweet little ninos."

I didn't turn to see if any were converging on me or the U-Haul. I was mesmerized by the little lady with the big chutzpa. A ring of screaming began. When they were all over her a wall of flame blew out in a broadening spiral. The things lit up and scattered, but she didn't stand there trembling. She *chased* them, round and round, as far as the hose would allow. Half a minute later she dropped the nozzle and let it burn. I floored us out of there and never looked back.

The little airport had been hit bad. It was burned out end to end, and bore a peculiarly ominous black-orange pall. Worse, that rotten egg stench was so bad it left us retching. And that shrill, steady whine upset the equilibrium; it was no longer just an annoying background noise, it was a very real and jangling pitch. Our eyes watered and our sinuses drained furiously.

We broke into the main office. While she watched the door I tore all the keys from their pegs and dropped them in a little tin pail behind the counter. We hurried on foot to the first row of two-seaters.

There was a protracted cooing behind the office. Another across the runway. In half a minute the stinking air was filled with calls and replies.

I rooted through the pail, chattering, "That one's labeled 72-A. And here's the keys, on this big old ring. One'll be the cockpit door, the other'll certainly be for the ignition. If this one doesn't work I've got a whole can of 'em." I fumbled the ring into her hands.

"What do you freaking want me to do with them?"

"What do you freaking think? Fly us the hell out of here!"

"Well, I hate to be a party-pooper, but I've never been in a plane in my life."

"Don't mess with me, man! You directed us here; *you led me on!* So what were you thinking? Like maybe you'd have your pick of bored pilots?"

She cuffed my forehead. "You're cute when you talk stupid. Don't worry. *Okay*, Violet? Papa was an air traffic controller. He told me all about it. All you have to do is hold onto the joystick with one hand and cross your heart with the other."

"Thank God for that. Well let's go, then. Just get us in the air and across the border. I'm not looking for a particularly smooth ride."

"And then what?"

"I dunno. Try to get things back to normal. Build us a homestead. Repopulate the race."

She looked like she wanted to heave. "What in hell would we name it?"

I thought for a bit. "If it's a boy, how's about Jack? And if it's a girl—"

She nodded ruminatively. "I've always liked Jill. Not too ethnic."

I grabbed the pail in one hand and her soft sweaty palm in the other. "Okay, Indiana. Here goes nothing."